# DARK DESIRE

## DARK DESIRES
### BOOK ONE

## SUMMER COOPER

LOVY BOOKS

# EMILY

"Emily, we'll be back around nine. Don't let the kids stay up too late." Jessi, my sister-in-law, said from the doorway to the living room.

As if her twin girls would ever listen to a thing I said. The door closed, and I turned to my twin nieces. "Who wants ice cream?"

The two little girls, identical blonde, sweet tyrants, screamed with joy as they looked back at me with gray eyes so similar to mine. They could be mine, if I wasn't so busy all the time. I pushed the thought away and stood up from the pillow fort they'd built around me to head into the kitchen.

Harry, the baby brother of the twins, slept in a playpen near the dark gray leather sofa, so I left him there. He was a growing boy, and he needed his sleep.

Soon enough he'd join his older sisters in the kitchen with me.

I found the girls on bar stools around the marble island in the kitchen. It was the kind of kitchen any baker would love. It was Jessi's kitchen, after all, and she needed three industrial sized ovens. I turned to the fridge, the same stainless steel as the oven, stove, and microwave, and asked which ice cream the girls wanted.

"I want strawberry, please, Aunty." Breanna, always the polite one, informed me sweetly.

"Yuck! I don't like strawberry! I would like rocky road, please." Rhiannon, the bossier of the two and always the most opinionated, cried out from her perch by her sister.

They were two peas in a pod, but they were also quite different when it came to their personalities. Even if they were identical.

"You two don't know how lucky you are to have a mother who's a baker," I muttered, more to myself than to them. I pulled out two cartons of ice cream from the freezer and a plate of brownies from the drawer above it. I microwaved the brownies for a minute and added the ice cream to each bowl, before I added a spoon and gave the bowls to the girls.

I'd only put in small amounts, the girls were still little after all, and sat with them, a small bowl of my own in front of me. "What movie are we going to watch, girls?"

The girls began to argue about which family-friendly movie they wanted to watch first, and my thoughts drifted. Jessi and Trent were off for a charity ball, and I'd been enlisted to watch the girls and baby Harry. I knew the routine. I'd helped with babysitting since the girls were first born and had also helped with my other nieces and nephews.

Over the last five years, what was a small family of three brothers and a sister, had turned into one huge family. I often spent time flying back and forth to watch the children who resulted from my brothers' unexpected, but totally welcome, romances. The hard men I'd barely known in my younger days had now become men with a softness around their hard edges, and I was a spinster.

I looked at the bowl in front of me, totally untouched, and imagined a candle on the top of it. The birthday song played in my head, and I had to swipe a tear away. How had all of them forgotten it was my birthday? I hadn't received a call from any of my brothers or my sisters-in-law. Even Trent and Jessi had forgotten about the event.

I'd kind of hoped that one of them would remember, that there'd been a surprise element to tonight's babysitting gig, but no. Just a charity event somewhere in downtown Myrtle Beach that they'd planned to attend.

Jessi had looked glorious in a black velvet gown, and Trent was always impressive in a tux.

I swiped at the blonde ponytail that had fallen over my shoulder and gave the girls a wan smile.

"What's wrong, Aunty?" little Rhiannon asked softly. She put her spoon down and put her tiny little hand on my cheek. "Do you have a sad?"

"I do, honey, but you two make it all better. And Harry, of course."

"Do you want to watch a grown-up movie instead of one of our movies?" Breanna added from her stool.

"No, honey, it's fine. Let's wash up the bowls and settle in. A nice long cuddle with you two will make it all better." I loved my siblings and their children, but sometimes, I wanted what they had for myself.

I didn't resent that I was the family's version of Mary Poppins. I just wanted them to recognize that three flights a week was too much, and that I needed time to myself. And to have my special dates noticed. I only really had one, after all; why had it been so hard to remember this year?

Jessi and Trent had a new baby to deal with, as did Mason and Laura. They'd adopted a lovely little girl a month ago to add to the two children they'd had previously. Ember and Kevin only had one child, a beautiful little version of Ember that they'd called Bridget after her mother. That still amused me, that Ember's real name was Bridget Jones.

I'd loved Ember from the moment I met her, and that voice? She was a wonder, but then all of my sisters-in-law were wondrous. Then there was me. The family caretaker and a spinster. What a life.

The girls surprised me and fell asleep twenty minutes into the movie. We'd piled up on the broad, black velvet couch in front of the large screen television, one on each side of me, and I was now stuck between them. I didn't want to wake them up, but my phone began to buzz. I struggled for a moment and wanted to scream when the phone almost fell off the edge of the end table, but I caught it.

I opened the screen to see a text from my friend, Roxie Simpson, on the screen.

<Hey, girl, happy birthday. Want to celebrate with me after my set?>

I grinned, the pain in my chest eased just a fraction. I thought about what to say, about what she offered, and decided that, yes, I did want to celebrate.

<Are you sure you want to party with an old woman like me? I'm twenty-seven now!>

The response was almost instantaneous, and I grinned wider.

<Shut up, you aren't old. You're only a few months older than me. Meet me at my apartment around ten?>

<I'll be there. I have to wait for Trent and Jessi to get back, then I'll be there.>

I felt a little better about life after that, and I couldn't wait to see what Roxie had in store. She wasn't the kind of person you'd associate with a woman of my class. My father owned hotel chains across the world, but she was one of the best friends I had. Now that Jessi was a wife and mother, I spent a lot of time with my best friend too busy to talk to me.

I'd met Roxie at a fundraiser I'd been part of. She'd helped to organize the event, and we'd hit it off. She'd been in a wonderful lavender suit that fit her form, but she'd looked classy and well put together with her makeup in place and her manners impeccable. I hadn't known she was a stripper until she told me. Exotic dancer, that's what she called it.

Only she wasn't just an exotic dancer, the woman had skills and had won competitions all over the country with her performances. She continued to perform, but in her spare time, she volunteered with the charity I'd become a part of. She worked at some kind of exclusive gentlemen's club, code for strip joint, but she'd alluded to the fact that it was far more than that.

I'd often wondered about those allusions, and exactly what Roxie did to earn her money. She lived in a nice apartment on the outskirts of Myrtle Beach and drove a nice car. She always looked impeccably dressed, unless she was at home, and then she'd put on jeans and a tank top, or shorts and sweaters. Basically, she was just like me, except I lived in a mansion, didn't really have a specific job, was rich, and the world was my oyster. She had to work for her money.

I wasn't judging her; that wasn't the problem at all. On the contrary, I was quite intrigued about Roxie's life. She said she found her routines to be an escape, and the other tasks she did; well, sexual gratification was always a good thing. I wouldn't know. But I wanted to.

I took the girls up to their bedroom, put them each in their little pink fairy princess beds, and left a night-light on for them. Jessi and Trent would be back soon, and I'd be on my way. I went downstairs to check on Harry, found him awake, and gave him a bottle while we waited.

"Your mommy and daddy will be home soon, my little love," I said to him as he stared up at me with eyes so like Trent's. Like mine.

I never had time to date or find a husband, but at night, when I was alone in my rooms at whatever hotel I called home for the moment, I'd think about my future. Right now, it looked empty and bleak. I wanted a family, and the look of happiness that my brothers now wore. I wanted a baby of my own and a family.

Or so I considered. I knew I wanted children, but maybe not right away? I grinned a little as I burped

Harry over my shoulder and felt his little snuffles fall back to snores. Such a tiny little being, and so sweet.

The problem was, I wanted that same sweetness for myself, but I also wanted some of the wildness that Roxie had told me about. Parties where everybody ended up naked, and the private rooms some of the patrons of the club rented for their own escapades. I wanted to know more about that world.

I wanted to explore it and find out what it was all about. I was more than ready to find out what happened in the world of the grownups. I might have been rich, but I was also very sheltered, and I wanted to tear that shelter down.

I'd formed a plan by the time Trent and Jessi came back to the house at nine. I headed back to the hotel, changed into an outfit I'd hidden away in my suitcase of secret wonders, and looked at myself in the mirror. I'd applied a little makeup, just enough to make the gray in my eyes lighter, and had curled my hair into long waves. The lace top, with a shelf bra to protect my modesty, and short white skirt spoke of my innocence, but left little to the imagination.

I added a pair of white heels, then left the room with a bag in hand. I went down to the parking garage, found the family car that was left there for any of us to use, and drove to Roxie's place. She let me in with a scream of excitement and a hug.

"Girl, it's been a month since I've seen you! How are you?" She offered me a drink, and we'd both sat by the time I got around to answering her.

"I've been rushed off my feet. I keep flying from place to place, and I tell you, I'm tired." I sipped at the wine she'd given me and set the glass on the table.

Her living room was done in white, glass, and gold trimmings. Tasteful but not gaudy. I didn't want to ruin her carpets with red wine if I got clumsy, so I'd asked for white wine.

"Why don't you tell them to hire a nanny, honey? You can't keep living like this."

I looked at her with a little guilt on my face before I smiled. "I told Trent tonight that I needed more time to myself, and I wouldn't be watching the kids so much. I need to be here to work on that project we've started, and I'll be around, but I won't be flying back and forth between Laura and Mason in Charlotte, and Kevin and Ember in Tennessee. I know they all want someone they trust around their kids, but you're right, Roxie. It's time for me to spread my wings." I left out the part where I wanted her to help me do just that. For now.

"Okay! Good for you! I'm glad you finally did that. It will be nice to have you around." She was two feet away on the other end of the white damask couch. I couldn't help but compare myself to her.

She wore a black leather bustier type top and black

leather pants, yet she still looked sophisticated. Maybe it was the black patent leather Prada kitten heels, the way her blonde hair was never out of place, or maybe it was the fact that Roxie never sweated, even in the heat, but she always looked so cool and collected, in control. I admired her. Those blue eyes helped too. They were so… bright.

I felt underdressed, and maybe a little trashy in my attempts at sexy but sophisticated. I looked down at my lace top, something I would never wear to any place my brothers or parents might see me, and wondered if it wasn't a childish choice. Something someone pretending to be sophisticated would pick.

If it was frumpy but stylish, then I could pick it out. A suit that leaned a little to the too tight was about as risqué as I usually went. This outfit was my first attempt to fit into Roxie's world, which was much different from my own. Even if her world was full of power, controlling that power, and money. Not so different from mine, but the power struggles flowed different ways.

"Right, girl," Roxie said as she nudged me with her manicured fingers. "What do you want to do for your birthday? Where do you want to go?"

I looked at her, my breath caught in my chest. I had a plan, a cunning one, if she'd play along with it. "I, uh, I want a favor from you. Please."

"Alright?" she said, a darkened eyebrow arched at me questioningly.

"I want you to take me to that club. The gentlemen's club. I want to see what it's like in there. What the men are like, what happens with the women. I really, really want to find out for myself."

Her ruby red lips twisted into an amused smirk, and her eyes looked at me with pride. "Oh, girl. You want the birthday of a lifetime, then?"

"I do. Badly. Please, will you take me?" I waited, my hands clenched together as she looked me over. She just had to say yes. It was my birthday, and she was the only one who remembered!

2

# DYLAN

"You're a descendent of Jesse James, aren't you?" a woman at the end of the conference table asked.

My gaze flicked to the woman, and I noted round, out of date glasses, fuzzy hair, and a little too much fluff around the hips. She had a twisted little mouth that looked cruel, and I wondered who she was and how she'd come to be here.

"I am, yes, in a way. I'm adopted, but the man who became my father is descended from his son, as a matter of fact." It wasn't a point of pride, just something I'd had to learn to deal with over the years. Every now and then someone would crop up to ask me if I had special knowledge about the gunslinging outlaw from long ago.

I was born in 1986, so how could I know anything about a man who died over 100 years before I was born?

It was a familiar question, though, and one I'd grown bored with long ago.

"He was such a handsome man," she crooned from the other end of the table, and I tried not to roll my eyes. The man had been a murderer and a thief; his spawn had tried to live good lives, despite their ignoble birth, and to get on with life. We didn't see him as a romantic hero, even if he had been handsome.

"I suppose if you consider murderous bank robbers handsome, well, I guess he was," I muttered and looked away. The woman I'd been waiting on, Liz Kearny, came in to the meeting room at last.

"Dylan James, as I live and breathe, how are you?" Her wide, red painted smile greeted me and hid the lust in her eyes. At forty-two, Liz was still a fine specimen of a woman, but she was married. I wasn't interested.

"I'm good, Liz, I'm good. I needed to speak to you about some property." I sat and indicated the seat across from me. I kept my voice low so the woman at the other end of the table wouldn't hear us.

"I know, your PA told us all about it. Excuse me." She paused, turned her head to the woman who had asked me about my ancestry, and called out to her, "Imogen, what did you find out about that land for Mr. James?"

"The land has been bought out by the Thompson family. I'm afraid, we're too late." She didn't even look down at the papers to verify what she'd said; she just knew her job and did it well.

"I thought that might happen. Liz, can't you find me something to work with here? Some way of getting them off my back? Or lawn, so to speak?" I gave her my most charming smile and added a gentle tease to my voice.

Her eyes went soft, and her face relaxed as I allowed my head to lean a little closer to her. It was a stupid ploy, but when you want something as much as I wanted to expand my resorts, Sky B-n-B, out here to Myrtle Beach, well, you did what was necessary. I'd wasted a lot of time already because I'd had to deal with things at Pebbles, the resort chain my adopted father had left me in charge of when he retired.

"I'll find you something. Something you can't turn down." Her voice was husky, and her eyes were like a laser focused on mine.

"I would appreciate that," I murmured seductively and let my tongue flick out to wet my lips.

My family had started a chain of hotels when great-great-whatever grand-daddy Jesse, Jr, had fathered a daughter. She had turned a boarding house into a string of hotels out in Kansas, and the coming generations expanded it west. By the time I came along, the family had a hotel in almost every single state in the west. Now, I wanted to move the family east, and Myrtle Beach was a hidden jewel I wanted to wrap in a platinum setting. I hadn't counted on the Thompson Hotel chain's resistance.

"I guess that's all we need to talk about for now. Thank you for the work you've done so far, Liz. I'll expect a call if you find something suitable." I stood, buttoned the panels of my suit coat, and made to leave.

"Oh, now, as your real estate agent, Dylan, I can't just let you leave empty-handed. I have a wonderful house going if you're looking for a private home on the waterfront." She started her spiel, and I shut her down.

"Not interested in that, just resort property. Take care now." I inhaled deeply as I left the room of one of the top estate agencies in the area, and made my way to the parking garage. I needed to relax. I'd been dealing with this family for two long months now, and I had deserved a break.

I decided to take the night off and head out to the gentlemen's club I'd been introduced to upon my arrival. I'd met up with an old friend, Freddy Sinclair, and he'd shown me the best parts of this wonderful little beach town. He'd also shown me the spots the tourists would never find out about.

Like Elmo's. The strip club/sex club I kept my nose out of kind of place. It was exclusive, kept quiet, and entry was by invite only, if you were a man or woman looking to partake in the custom Elmo's had to offer.

I liked the finer things in life, and the girls at Elmo's were of the highest caliber; I'd give them that. I hadn't found exactly what I wanted there yet, but I knew patience would pay off. It always did.

I made it to the club and walked in the secluded entrance in the back. From the front, the place looked like an abandoned store with three levels. Red paint covered every square inch, and the place looked like a gaudy dump. It didn't look much better in the back; all of the windows and every surface had been painted black. There was a shiny new gold knob on the door, however, and I put my hand on it but didn't turn.

Beneath the round knob was a palm scanner. If it accepted your palm print, the door would open on its own, as it did now. "Welcome, Mr. James."

The door person was a rather breathy and busty brunette, but she was off-limits. "Thank you, Miss Maples. Lovely to see you again."

"A pleasure as always. What will it be today?" The owner of the club didn't often sit and guard the door, but sometimes she could be found here.

"I just need a quiet place to watch some beautiful ladies dance their hearts out." It wasn't a past-time I'd take part in back home in Kansas, but here, I'd learned to live a little on the wilder side.

I could be me here, with all of my proclivities and vices.

"Enjoy the show; Roxie's on in ten." Miss Maples turned away even as she spoke, my presence already forgotten as someone else buzzed in.

I ordered a drink at the bar and sat. The shoddy exterior, designed to keep out curious onlookers, did not match the interior. The first floor housed a bar, a stage, and a small club on the other side of that. The club was a separate part of the first floor, one I rarely went into because I wasn't into rave-style hedonism. I was much too old for that crowd.

I preferred the darkness of the stage area and to watch the pole dancing magic. Roxie would be on soon, and I wanted to speak to her anyway. I'd noticed her quite a few times, but I hadn't spoken to her yet. I wanted to know if we could, perhaps, take part in one of the peculiar arrangements available at Elmo's.

I watched her go through her routine, effortless beauty, stunning grace, and skills beyond measure on display. Roxie never disappointed her viewers, and the tips she brought in proved that. She started a new routine, and I waited, my interest growing. If she could move like that on a pole, how well could she move on a man?

Sexist, perhaps disgusting, but people didn't come to Elmo's to find love; they came to relax, get turned on, and maybe fuck, if they were lucky. I saw Freddy, the man who had introduced me to the place, and wondered… Was he Roxie's protector now?

Freddy was a very handsome man, I'd give him that, and he'd never had problems with women. Those brown puppy dog eyes and blond hair kept the ladies on a leash, begging to take care of him. I, on the other hand, had black hair, dark gray eyes and was so tall and broad women often found me intimidating. If the broadness had been fat, it might have softened my appearance a bit, but every inch of me was covered in muscle. I worked hard to maintain my health, and I didn't allow an ounce of fat to form on me.

I didn't often have a problem finding a bed partner, though; there were plenty of women brave enough to take the challenge I offered them. Women with eyes that gave off sparks of defiance, that eventually ended up begging for me to make them mine. I never did, though. The minute their will broke, I was done and moved on to the next. A handsome face made that much easier.

I wanted Roxie, but if she was under Freddy's protection, then I'd have to look elsewhere. A dainty blonde, small and delicate, caught my eye. She had on a silky emerald robe that flowed out behind her as she walked around the room, in search of a man to entertain. There were about eleven other customers in the room, but she didn't spend much time with any of them.

She flitted around, nervous, with a fear in her eyes. I

would guess it was that fear that drove the men to send her away. Nobody wanted an unwilling partner. That was the cost of protection after all. The arrangement was about sex, and nothing more. We would pay to protect the ladies, in a sense, and in exchange, we were free to enjoy each other. We were all adults, however, and knew that arrangement meant sex.

If the woman wasn't into a guy, then she could turn him down, no problem. Most arrangements were made through Miss Maples or Roxie. It was all done in a way to protect all involved, from all manners of problems, and could be ended without notice to either party. Maybe this woman would do that for me? If we could get rid of that fear.

"Hello there, gorgeous," she said softly as she made her way up to me. I looked her over, noted the sweet swell of large breasts beneath the panels of the robe and a slim waist too. The perfect little doll for me to play with, maybe.

"What's your name, angel?" We all knew the women used fake names, but we played along. They needed their privacy and dignity, after all.

She wore a white mask, a wide ribbon of silk with the eyes cut out so they could see. The white looked almost silver it was so shimmery, and on this young woman, it made her appearance more tantalizing while enabling her to remain anonymous. All the girls in training wore them as a way to let customers know they were new, and as a way for them to maintain their dignity until they were sure this was the life they wanted. That strip of silk would allow her to return to her life without anyone knowing what she looked like without it.

"Why, I think you just gave it to me." She spoke with a deep Southern accent, the kind that made my balls go tight. Sweet, submissive, and so sultry.

"Indeed? Would you like to sit?" Her eyes had darted around nervously, her hands clasped together until she sat. She relaxed the moment she did, and I wondered if the heels had pained her. Six-inch heels were hard for any woman to stand in.

"How long have you been here, angel?" I asked and flicked a hand toward the bartender. A waitress brought over a glass of the beer I'd been drinking and a glass of wine for the lady.

"It's my second day, but I've been a pole dancer for three years now. I came up from Georgia just to check out the scene." She didn't look much older than twenty-three, I noted as I looked her over. She had pretty brown eyes, straight but large white teeth, and a lovely smile. It was just a shame her chin was a little too long and her nervousness hadn't completely receded.

I could look past those problems, if she'd calm down a little more. Let me see who she really was and what she really wanted from life. Some of the girls who came to Elmo's came to seek fame. They wouldn't find it here. They might find a protector who would help them find it, but fame didn't come from Elmo's.

It was an exclusive, prestigious place, but the ultimate goal wasn't to propel a dancer to stardom; it was to provide men, and some women, with sexual partners. This little angel wasn't going to last long here, I was afraid.

"I guess you'll learn to fit in then. It's still early. You might settle in just fine." It wasn't proper to ask a woman how she ended up at Elmo's, but one thing was certain, they were there under their own free will. Some had even found protectors who moved them out into their own newly-purchased houses and put them on an annual income.

That was the ultimate goal here, to never have to work again. Not a "real" job, anyway. Mistresses for hire, that was what the place boiled down to.

"I guess I will." She sipped at her wine prettily and looked at my chin, not my eyes. Hers flicked up to mine for an instant and then shied away. It wasn't an act, I decided; she was afraid.

"You know you don't have to do anything you don't want to right? You're perfectly free to dance if that's all you want to do." I'd been versed on the rules well and warned about repercussions if I didn't follow those rules. No meant no, and anything other than acceptance would get a patron banned.

"I know, but I thought I'd try. At least once, you know? I've never done that before, just slept with a man for money."

"It's awkward, I assume, for you ladies?" I hadn't really thought about it. Most of the women I'd met here had been eager, curious to find out what hid behind the cool façade.

I was sure more than one would be amused to find me with the kitten who had found herself lost in the big, bad world. I didn't want to turn her away, because she might prove to be exactly what I wanted.

"It is, but most of the women here want to sleep with the men they choose. It's not like we have to do it. They want to. I just haven't found a man I want to do it with yet."

"Then, I suggest you wait for the right one, angel. There's no rush." I smiled and sat back as Roxie began another set.

It was almost nine, and she'd be done soon. I'd talk to her and then go home, I decided. It had been a long day, and I'd only found disappointment so far. Maybe a night's sleep would cure that.

# EMILY

"What about these, Roxie? They'd look great on you!" I called Roxie over to me, and she stared at the colorful pair of heels I'd stopped at in the boutique I'd brought us to.

My birthday had been and gone a week ago, and Roxie still hadn't told me if she could get me into the club she worked at. We'd spent my birthday in her apartment, watching our favorite movies and getting drunk. It had been fun, a first rebellion, and I'd passed out on her couch around one a.m. Since then, we'd both been busy with different things, but we'd finally met up for a shopping trip that I'd proposed.

She'd wanted to head over to the discount shops along the boardwalk, but I'd driven us to a secluded set of boutiques just outside of town. She'd been confused but hadn't protested. I liked that about Roxie; she was brave, curious, and wasn't afraid of much in the world.

"God, put those back, Emily; I can't afford them," Roxie whispered to me as I picked up a pair of Christian Louboutin shoes. I looked up at her confused.

"But I have this?" I put the shoes down, dug around in my bag, opened my wallet and showed her a Platinum Visa card. I'd never had to worry about things such as prices in my entire life. I just bought what I want and used the card Daddy gave me when I was thirteen. Sometimes, I felt guilty about the fact that I had an unlimited amount of credit to spend, but, except for clothes and dining out, I rarely used the thing. Besides, since the children came along, I'd barely bought any new clothes, and dining out wasn't something I did often either.

"Jesus is that…" Roxie's eyes went wide as she looked down at the card. "Fuck me, it is."

"What?" I asked; didn't everybody have credit cards these days?

"An unlimited platinum credit card, Emily? I've heard about them, but I've never actually seen one." I could see Roxie reassessing me when she looked up at me.

She knew I was a Thompson, but had she not realized how much money we had? I felt my cheeks flame and moved away. We were here to buy some new outfits for me to wear when I set my plan in motion; though, she didn't quite know it yet. I'd wanted to buy her something too, but she kept refusing everything I showed her.

"It's no big deal. Do you want them?" I lifted a blonde eyebrow and grinned at her with a look that teased. "Go on, try them on at least."

"Well…," I saw her cheeks flush and knew I'd won her over to the platinum club.

"Go on … have the sales lady bring you a pair. It'll be my treat." I really wanted her to have them and felt glad when she finally gave in.

She ran off to find the woman with the sour look on her face. Roxie, in her bright pink, form-fitting bandage dress and hot pink heels, obviously hadn't been to the woman's liking. Fuck her, I thought. I picked out a pair of shoes for myself. They were black patent leather with peep toes that would be a nightmare to walk in, but they'd look so sexy on my feet.

Another pair caught my eyes, another peep-toe stiletto, but this one had been covered in white graffiti over the black patent leather. Something about it drew me, and I reached for that one while I bit at my bottom lip unconsciously, wondering if I should be so very … extravagant. I looked up to see Roxie twisting in front of a mirror, the gaily colored shoes on her feet. Yeah, I should start my rebellion now, I decided.

I picked up both sets and asked the woman to bring

me the shoes in my size. She looked me up and down, noted the obvious signs of money, and demurred quite respectfully. Bitch.

"Is there anything else you want?" I asked Roxie, as we'd sat on a pair of cushions in the small shop. There wasn't much to choose from, but this was one of those places that usually only kept a few things on a rack and brought you the size you asked for. If they had it in your size.

"Not from here. Are you serious? You're going to buy these for me?" Her face was shocked, hopeful, but I could also see a spark that said she couldn't accept the gift.

"Look, my family is rich; I can't help that. But I can make your day, if you'll let me. I hate spending money on myself, but for you, I'd love to spend the money that I'll never be able to spend entirely from my share of the family income."

"Are you sure want to do this?" Suddenly, I knew she wasn't talking about the shoes, and I tensed. She hadn't forgotten then. My heart skipped a beat with anticipation; would she say yes, finally?

"I dream about it, Roxie." I followed her lead and said it softly, so we wouldn't be overheard. "I feel as if I've lived in a bubble my entire life. I want to know what it *feels* like outside of the walls my family has built around me. You can help me with that. I wouldn't trust anyone else to do it."

"I think I understand. I've had to think about it a lot, but I think, maybe, I can get you in."

"A maybe is somewhere. How did it go this week anyway?" Roxie had a new client, a very well-off man who wanted to become her protector. The thing was, Roxie didn't really need one. She earned a good living as a professional pole-dancer, and her gig at Elmo's was just to tide her over until the next competition and more prize money.

"He asked to be my protector again." She sighed, and for the thousandth time, I wondered what it would be like to have sex with a man who paid you for the privilege.

Oh, I knew the rules: the woman has to be agreeable, the woman has to set ground rules, and the man has to abide by them. But still, the man … owned you, in a way, and that thought excited me more than I'd ever admit to anyone. Even now, just the thought of it had stirred a heat in my blood.

"Are you going to agree?" I knew she didn't have to, but this client seemed different. Roxie didn't usually keep a man at the club for more than a week or two, but this one, he had some thrall over her. Maybe she'd met her match, finally?

"I don't know. I think, maybe…," she paused and

looked around but there were no answers on the bright white walls, only cubby holes filled with shoes. "I think I might."

"Oh my." My eyes went round, but I settled my face when the woman came back with the shoes I'd asked for. I looked them over, tried them on, and agreed to both pairs. And the pair Roxie had on.

The shop lady looked over at Roxie and then to me. "As you wish."

Something about that really irked me, and I wanted to demand to know what the woman's problem was. Roxie might be showy, but she wasn't trash. This woman didn't know how hard Roxie worked for the children's charity or the hours she spent on drumming up financial resources for the charity. She just assumed Roxie was a strumpet, I guessed, and treated her accordingly. I hated people sometimes.

"I'd like to punch her right in that puckered-up mouth of hers," Roxie whispered, and I laughed far too loudly.

"I think you'd break your hand on that stone wall she calls a face." The woman brought my card back, I signed the slip, and we took our purchases to the next boutique.

There, I bought a few skin-tight dresses of my own and some new underwear. Sexy panties and bras were a weakness of mine, and I bought Roxie a few too. She tried on one of the bras before we bought them, and she asked me how it looked before she'd agree to let me buy it.

"I don't want to see your boobs!" I squawked from behind the door.

"Look, I'm not trying to hit on you; I just want to know you're happy with what you've bought." I could hear a throaty tease in that voice, and I knew she was probably smirking behind that door.

Roxie and I were friends, but she knew I was just a little … uptight. Undressing in front of each other was usually unnecessary in our time together, but it had happened before, and she always teased me about what a prude I was.

"Come on, have a look. It won't kill you." I heard from the other side of the door.

"Fine!" I whispered loudly and opened the door. Roxie was a lovely woman, with a beautiful figure, and her body reflected her fitness regime. Her breasts, surgically augmented, looked much better than mine did in the same powder blue lace bra. Mine were smaller, but nice, I guessed.

"How does it look?" she teased and winked at me.

"It looks like I need a boob job!" We both giggled, the tension gone as we laughed together.

"Well, I can tell you, don't go this big." Roxie

squeezed her forearms around the globes on her chest and rolled her eyes. "It's such a pain."

"I wouldn't know." I laughed with her as she turned, replaced her bra, and put her dress back on before we left the changing rooms.

We finished shopping and left to go eat at one of her favorite places. It was a quiet little burger place, but I loved it. Nobody cared how much money I made; they only wanted to know if the food was good and went on to the next customer. We talked about our project for a while and worked on some plans for fundraising. But, like always, our talk eventually turned to Roxie's job. She had to go soon to get ready for her night at work.

I wanted to beg her to take me with her, but she hadn't said yes yet. I wouldn't push; I knew something like that would take time. She couldn't just drag anybody off the street in there. It was exclusive not only in the individuals who were allowed in, but who came to work there. I'd have to go through some kind of process, I was sure.

We said our goodbyes, and I drove back to my room at the hotel. I'd wanted to get my own place, my own apartment, but hadn't got around to it yet. If I stuck with my promise to take more time for myself, I'd invest in a place where my house plants wouldn't die because I wasn't around to water them. Until then, I'd stay at the hotel.

Maybe I'd even buy myself an RV, and travel around, see the country a little. In time, I thought as I sank into my bed after a shower. For now, I wanted to experiment. I thought about Roxie and what she did. What did it feel like to have a stranger touch you? Was it frightening? Was it empowering?

Did she watch those men, weak with desire for the body she loved, feel like she was the one with all the power, all the control? Did they beg to touch her? To kiss her? I hummed without meaning too, something alive all over again in my body. In the darkness, flat on my back, my legs opened, and I wondered … what would it feel like?

I'd been tempted to buy toys, to find out for myself, but had decided the real thing was worth waiting for. I turned my head toward the window, but I didn't see anything. My sight was internal, caught on an image of a man flat on his back as he waited for me to … do things. I swallowed hard and tried to imagine what it would be like to do the things I'd seen in videos online.

I'd watched a lot of videos in the spare time I had at night. With my headphones on, my doors locked, and my laptop on the bed beside me, I'd watched the many things people could do together. Some of it was just nasty and degraded all involved, others had looked exciting, sensual, and some of it had seemed hedonistic.

Some of it, well … some of it was obviously the

result of people losing all control and had seemed wildly erotic. I'd gone through lists: lesbian sex, straight sex, orgies, doms and subs; classic porn and new porn, some even labeled "ladies porn", meant for the discerning woman. I'd watched it all, and I'd found a lot of it intriguing, but maybe not for me. I always went back to one category, no matter what, though.

The ones where the women were subs to others. I liked the women who were subs to other women, and the women who were subs to men. It was the sub part that attracted me. The look of pure joy on their faces as they served intrigued me far more than anything else did. It wasn't something I'd ever tell to anyone; it was my secret, this need inside of me to be in control through subservience.

You'd think with the way I had lived my life in servitude to my family that I'd want to be the domme in this situation, but I didn't. I wanted to be totally without shame, begging for release, as my body sang with life. I wanted my control to be in an expert's hands, not my own. Maybe then I'd find freedom, though an odd form of it, I'd admit.

This wasn't something I'd decided on suddenly. I'd thought about it for quite a few years now, and when I'd met Roxie and she told me about her club, I'd known I'd finally found a way into the world I'd been locked out of. Her world would be my world soon.

4

---

# DYLAN

"**W**hat's your poison?" the bartender asked, and I stared dully at the man. A long brown beard adorned his face, tight khaki pants clashed with the sophisticated haircut, and for some unknowable reason, suspenders over a white t-shirt with Pink Floyd emblazoned across the front. The whole look, clashed in my mind, and I stared at him.

Then a word popped into my head, and I relaxed. Hipster. "Beer please, thanks."

He gave me a nod, passed along a beer, and I headed off in the direction of the stage. I had spent another day fruitlessly looking for land to develop. At this point, I'd even take a large house that I could turn into apartments, though, small ones. I wanted to be in this place, this part of the world, to get away from my life in Kansas.

I needed to be away from it all, but I wouldn't get that, not until someone else came along to take the lead from me. My own child or someone I took under my wing. I might yet find a wife, settle down, have a child, but I didn't see it coming. Not yet.

I was only thirty-two, I'd have time; I reminded myself as I took a seat. Roxie was on the stage, weaving her magic as always. The woman was amazing to watch, I'd give her that. I looked around and appreciated the décor, yet again. It wasn't trashy, the kind of place you'd expect it to be from the exterior. It was done tastefully, even if it was decorated in the cliché black and red colors that are so prevalent in such places.

The place was clean too; there was always someone going around discreetly with a bottle of disinfectant and roll of paper towels to clean up spills of all kinds. The tables and chairs were replaced if damaged, and not a chip was to be found on table tops. The paint was kept fresh, and everything was neat.

It was, however, dark, always dark. You could see to walk, it wasn't like being in a cave in total blackness, but it was dark. The lights were saved for the stage. My eyes went back to Roxie, and I admired the way she climbed up the pole, performed a few twisting moves then made her way down the steel rod.

She was dressed in a pair of black hot pants, black combat boots, and a black corset. I didn't know the song, but it had a powerful, frantic rhythm that drove her frenzied on the stage. She had the full attention of everyone in the room, there was no doubt of that. The routine came to an end, and applause and cheers filled the room.

It was 8:15 pm. Most of these men were single or had wives who stopped asking where their husbands spent their nights long ago. Freddy was there, and Roxie left the stage to join him with a smile. She saw me and quirked an eyebrow.

I twitched my glass at her and gave her a smile. She said something to Freddy and headed in my direction.

"Angel wasn't for you then?" she asked and sat beside me at the table.

"No, too unsure of what she wanted. Poor girl, I think she's left the place now."

"She did, that's why I asked. I thought she'd be your type?" We'd discussed the kind of arrangement I'd like to have, after I learned she was definitely taken by Freddy, and she'd kept an eye out for me.

"She would have been, if she had been able to make up her mind. She couldn't, so I let it go. I need someone who knows what she wants, because I plan to give it to her." I didn't go into detail; we'd talked about it before. She knew what I wanted. A woman who would give me everything she had and then pull out a little more to give.

There wasn't necessarily a manager here at Elmo's but if there was a problem, or a question needed to be answered, your best bet was to talk to Roxie, I'd learned. She drew a lot of the members to come back night after night, but she'd been unattainable for most, and the ones who had her didn't keep her for long. Until Freddy.

"Well, I might know someone who will meet your needs, but she's not here yet." Roxie's green eyes watched me, appraising. "I think she's ready for a place like this; she says she is, but I have to be sure. She's not, hmm."

Roxie paused, looked away as if lost in thought, and then came back to me. "She's not the usual kind we bring into this place. We're a classy place, don't get me wrong, but most of the women we bring know exactly what life's about. They decide to come here knowing what it is they'll get. I need to be sure she's ready for that. She's had an easy life, and well, I think she wants to start breaking her boundaries."

"Oh?" I asked and leaned closer. "What's her kind then?"

"Pampered," she said immediately, and then felt guilty; I could see it in the way she winced. "She's a good friend of mine, but she's had a very sheltered and privileged life."

"I see." I sat back and tapped on the table top. I wasn't sure that I wanted a daddy's girl who wanted to rebel. I wanted a pet, yes, a woman to bend to my will until she had the best orgasm of her life, and I'd done that many times already, but did I want to start out with a spoiled princess?

It would be a lot of work. "She'd be worth it."

Roxie had already piqued my interest, but that assurance from her was guaranteed to get my full attention. "And why would you bring such a woman to a place like this? If she's your friend?"

"Because she needs it. Maybe more than anyone else I've ever met. She needs what you have to offer. I lived that life a long time ago, and I'm well past it now, but my friend… She might be the kind who lives the lifestyle for life. She's a giver, and she can't change that about herself, no matter how hard she might try."

"I see." I tapped again, lost in thought. "Can you bring her in?"

"I'm arranging it. If she can make it through the doors, I think she'll be just what you're looking for."

"Alright." She must want something out of this, and I was blunt enough to ask her what it was. "Why me? Why are you offering your friend up to me?"

"Because, dear sir, you have that look in your eye. Like you want to break a woman, but in a good way, not the bad way. And my little friend needs just that. She's so hungry for it, she's on the verge of losing control. I think you can teach her that control. In all, I believe you're the perfect teacher for her. She's liable to get into trouble if she's not guided in the right direction. Also, I know I can have you killed if you break her the wrong way." The note of jest in her voice was belied by the promise in her eyes.

"I understand." I meant her reasons for offering up her friend and the warning. I believed she'd do it too, if the intensity of that gaze was anything to go by.

"I propose you speak with her, let her settle in to the place, and then make your offer. Don't pounce the moment you see her; take your time, and let her decide. Then, you will likely find you've found far more than you bargained for."

I nodded in agreement. This wasn't my first rodeo, and I knew how to break a filly properly, how to make her bend to your will. Now, if I could only find some property out here too, that would be the icing on the cake.

"Thank you, Roxie." For the first time, I wondered if that was her real name, but I didn't ask. There were some things you left alone in a place like Elmo's. Names was one of those things.

"My pleasure. And remember, you break her wrong, I break you." Her well-manicured eyebrows lifted over sharp green eyes, and I felt a shiver run down my back. I'd have loved to make those eyes flicker with challenge, but she was taken.

"I like breathing and living above ground, Roxie. I'll be gentle. I promise." I'd be as gentle as the kitten offered to me wanted me to be, and no more gentle than that.

I wouldn't tell Roxie that, however. What happened between the woman and I was only for us to know. I knew I had to tread carefully, though. Freddy was definitely the kind of man who likely knew a few of the less nefarious types who crawled along the underbelly of Myrtle Beach.

I wondered what she looked like, this paragon that Roxie wanted to deliver to me. I'd wait, let the curiosity build. Roxie grabbed my attention when she stood up, bent down to kiss my cheek, and left me.

I had something to think about anyway.

A day of scouring websites and driving around to view properties had left me a little cranky, and I decided to change to scotch. I'd get a cab back to my place later. I went to the bar and ordered my drink.

Miss Maples came into the bar as I waited and sidled up next to me. "Good to see you again, Mr. James. How are you?"

"I'm alright, Miss Maples. Lovely to see you again." I tilted the glass with two cubes of ice at her, and she smiled.

She was a very seductive woman, especially in that corset wrapped around a gossamer robe. Her hip bumped against mine, and I looked down into her darkly lined eyes. Her skin said she was only in her late twenties, but I knew plastic surgery could make that a lie. A person didn't come to own a business like this at such a young age. Unless they made a lot of money early in life and spent it wisely. She could be as young as her face said she was, but then again, maybe not.

"You aren't finding much luck here, it would seem." She sat on a bar stool so I sat with her.

"Not yet, but I'm a patient man." I nodded, and I scanned her with my eyes while she ordered a drink.

Firm, high breasts said her face didn't lie, and her hands were still full with the promise of youth. She had the kind of fingers made for pianos or guitars, but I'd never heard her play anything. A lush figure, encased in that corset promised heaven most people would never be lucky enough to find.

I'd been surrounded by beautiful women for days now, all with the promise of sex so near, but yet, just out of reach for one reason or another. I was about ready to take the first lay offered to me, but I'd wait. I wanted to be clean for this little present Roxie offered me.

"She'll come along. Maybe before you know it." She sipped at her red wine, her eyes on mine over the rim of her glass.

"So I've been told." I didn't elaborate, and she didn't ask me to, so I let it go.

"What else is there to do in this place?" I asked, and she gave me an amused smile.

"Care to walk with me through the dungeon?" I had no idea what she meant, but I was intrigued. Perhaps this was the rumored room on the third floor. I'd heard about it, but I hadn't seen it yet.

It was for the exhibitionist members of the club, those who got off on being watched. Not necessarily my style, but it might be interesting to walk through such a place with Miss Maples. She finished her wine, and I threw back the rest of my scotch.

"I would love to join you, Miss Maples." I held my elbow out, and she took it without another word. We headed to the elevator I'd yet to use, and she inserted a card she'd pulled from beneath her corset into the slot in the elevator panel. "We need a card to get up there?"

"No, but we're not going up. You need a card to go down." She gave me another enigmatic smile, and my eyes narrowed on her. This was interesting.

The floor rushed down, and before I knew it, the doors opened up to a world of black. A real dungeon, perhaps? The flicker of flames on the wall caught my eyes as I stepped out, and she joined me. Her hand was still on my elbow, and she took a step forward. I followed, not sure where to head.

She took me down a long hallway, lit with gas lamps on the wall, a very old-fashioned but very romantic way to light an area. We walked down a white carpeted hall, and I found myself in a world where sound disappeared. There were no footsteps, no sound from the gas lamps on the wall, no sounds from the rooms that I found myself peering into.

There was a row of rooms here, all with a door, but large glass panels for walls. Inside the first room I saw a bare, rock floor and a couple who was completely oblivious to their new audience. A woman in shiny black vinyl whispered to a man chained to a wall. He looked the banker type, the kind of man who ruled with an iron fist all day long. His belly was soft, and his hair had receded. His body trembled now as the woman's face brought him to a quivering mass of subservience.

Interesting, and a direction I found interesting, but I wasn't the kind to let anyone control me. "Hmmm, not your thing."

"No, but it is nice to watch, Miss Maples." I didn't mind watching at all. The woman was an expert at what she offered; I could see that from the way she'd wrung the man out already.

"Allana is good; I'll give you that." She breathed in deep and then tugged at my arm. "Come along."

We moved then to a room of white, lit by more gas lamps. The bed was white, the walls, the floor, even the hangings on the four poster bed were white. The only spot of color came from the two women on the bed.

They touched tenderly, sweetly, and I wanted to watch, but this wasn't what I wanted either.

"I think this is more your style, Mr. James." Her throaty voice all but purred.

A woman in a room of black, naked except for a mask across her eyes and the black silk around her wrists. A man with a crop stood over her, and I stopped. Yes, this was more my style. Definitely.

5

EMILY

*D*ays passed, and I hadn't heard from Roxie, but that might have been my own fault. I'd been busy. I finally found a place of my own, a real house, that was all mine. It was an exclusive place with a keypad on the large steel gate that kept the huge fence around the place locked up tight. I'd been busy buying furniture and a car.

I've never owned a car before, or furniture, but there was a first time for everything, right? I spent a week getting the place set up, and then, I finally talked to my family in a conference call on Skype. At first, there'd been confusion.

"But, Emily, we love you. What is this about?" Trent asked from his camera, and I glared.

"You love me?" I shot back, my face red with anger and hurt. "Or am I just convenient? Do any of you know

I'm a real human being?"

"Emily! What a thing to ask! Of course, we know you're real," Mason started, but I interrupted him.

"When is my birthday?" I asked pointedly, looking straight into the camera on my phone.

The three of them muttered across the screen on my phone, and I just smiled grimly. "It was last week. Trent, you didn't even remember when you asked me to watch the kids. You just thanked me for watching them and said goodbye because you were too exhausted to even sit with me for a little while."

"I'm, Emily, I'm very sorry." I heard contrition in his voice, but it didn't help.

"Emily, I can't believe I forgot, honey. I'm just, wow … sorry, babe." That from Kevin, the brother closest to my age.

Mason muttered his own apology, and I could see from his face he meant it. That didn't change the fact that things like this happened often, but every single one of them knew how to contact me when they wanted something. "From now on, you'll have to find a nanny or babysitter to take care of the children. I'd like to have some of my own one day, and if I'm constantly looking after yours, I won't find a man to do that with."

They all murmured in agreement and looked ashamed. So they should, I thought to myself. I'd given them a lot of my life, all of it up until now, and for once, it was time to think of myself. "I'm not walking out of your lives completely. I'm just asking for some space of my own. Surely you all understand that?"

"Well, yes, it was part of the reason I spent so much time in England before Ember came along," Kevin said quickly, in support.

"Kevin's right. I had my own place in the mountains, far away from our real lives until Dad pulled his shenanigans." That came from Trent.

"I used to party to escape. I partied all over the world. You've never done anything like that, Emily. I see your point now. You've had to take care of three brothers all this time. I support your decision too."

"Thank you." The conversation had ended soon after, but I did get calls from the wives. All of them were contrite too and supported my plans.

I needed to make roots somewhere, and I needed to be out of the Thompson loop. I didn't want to break all ties with my family; I just wanted time to live, to breathe, where I didn't have to worry that I'd have to fix some catastrophe or another that my brothers had created.

Now, I was in my own home with a car in the garage, and I counted myself lucky. The income I had from the family business, an income my father had set up on the day I was born, paid the huge amount of money I'd just spent on my new life. I sent Roxie a message and waited for her reply.

We agreed to meet, and I gave her directions to my new home.

"Wow, this place is nice, Emily!" She walked around the living room and kitchen with me, and I showed her the pool in the back. It was heated, so I could use it even in the cooler months. Then I took her to the upper floor.

"I've only decorated one of the bedrooms, right now. I have … plans for the other rooms," I stumbled and didn't know what to say that would reveal too much.

"I get it," she said and patted my arm as I showed her the empty rooms and the upstairs bathroom. There was one in my bedroom and another downstairs, so there were plenty of those.

The tour took the pressure off of me to explain that I wanted to turn one into an office, one room into a nursery one day, and one into a playground for me. And the baby's daddy.

The baby part could wait; I wasn't in a huge rush about that. I was hoping Roxie would help me with the getting-the-man part.

"It's a beautiful house, Emily, it really is." She smiled and hugged me. "You're getting there."

"I am. I told them all finally that I'm done playing super-nanny. I'll watch the kids from time to time, but right now, I need this."

She understood, she always had. When I met her at the office for the charity, I hadn't known what she did for a living, not at first. We worked together to help blind children learn how to live in a world without sight. Sometimes the children had been born blind, and sometimes it came as a result of illness, but either way, we were there to help them. I'd come to know her as a planner, a fellow fundraiser, and as a woman before I found out what she did. I didn't judge her career choices and never would. In fact, I rather admired those choices. I'd wished I'd been as brave long ago.

"I just need one more thing to help me along." I clasped my hands in front of myself and scrounged up the nerve to ask Roxie the one thing I wanted to know the most. "Can I come to the club with you?"

"Ah, I thought you'd get around to that eventually. Do you have coffee?" She looked at me with a grin, and I nodded as I led her downstairs. I wanted to pause and jump with joy, because I knew she had decided to let me go, but I didn't want her to change her mind either, so I ushered her down the stairs and into the kitchen.

"I'm not finished with unpacking yet, but I do have coffee available." I began the process of making coffee in a French Press, the only way I knew to make it, and wondered if I should use the coffee maker I'd bought. I didn't know how to use one and had left the machine in the box, on the counter since I'd moved in.

She told me about the things I'd have to do before I could apply: get a health check, blood tests, things like that, and that I'd have to speak with her boss. "If you can pass all of that, and I'm sure you can, then I don't think she'll have a problem letting you in."

"I just had a checkup done, so I can get that all emailed to me today." It was Friday, though, so I'd have to hurry to talk to someone. "Give me a minute."

I called the office and spoke with my doctor's receptionist. Within minutes I had the test results and printed them out. "What else do I need?"

"A background check, do you have a copy from when we had to provide them to Helping Hands?" Helping Hands was the nonprofit organization we volunteered with. Since we worked with children, we all had to have criminal background checks.

"I do, I made sure to get extra copies, just in case I needed them again this year." I had that in a folder upstairs. "What else?"

"Well, that's all I think." She looked over the test results and nodded. "Yes, I think that's all."

"Then I'm in?" I sat across from her at the little table in the kitchen that had sold me on the place.

I loved the pool, the bedrooms, the fact that I had so much room, and so many windows, but the kitchen had sold me. Along the back wall were cabinets above and below, a massive double sink, a gas stove top with a large oven against the right wall. Done in light wood and stainless steel, the kitchen was a dream. The fridge stood off to itself against the right wall, but that was fine. An island separated the utility area from a dining area, and I'd put in a pine table and four chairs to fill the space. A dining room was just off from the kitchen, but I doubted I'd ever really use it. Not for a while, at least.

I was excited, ready to go right now, but I had to hear her say the words before I'd let myself believe it was true.

"Look, this isn't just some brothel," Roxie began, her face full of her concern for me. "I know you have some kind of wish to find out what it's like, but I want you to know the reality of it. You can say no, at any time, to anyone. You aren't going to be forced to do anything. Right now, you can't perform on the stage, but if my boss agrees, you can act as a hostess. And if you find a patron you like, then you can discuss him becoming your protector."

"Okay. How long does that take?" From what she'd said, I knew the men were handsome, mainly alpha type, but some not so alpha. I wanted one who knew how to control a woman, how to make her feel alive.

"As long as you want it to take. You can go in tonight and find the perfect one. In fact, I might know someone." I saw how apprehensive she was, so I leaned in closer to her.

"What does he look like?" I asked, my eyes wide with anticipation.

"Like I'd have him if I hadn't accepted Freddy as my protector." She breathed the words, and I knew he must be gorgeous. "He's so fucking gorgeous."

"Roxie, you rarely swear," I noted, then grinned. "He must be super-hot."

"He's got a package in those pants of his you wouldn't believe too. I wish I'd been able to have a chance with him, but oh well. I think he'll be just right for you."

"We can go tonight?" I pushed, eager to know if I needed to get ready or not.

"Let me make a call, and I'll let you know. Bring me your background check, and I'll take pictures to send to my boss. We can take in the printouts to her later."

"Done!" I exclaimed with glee, and I ran up the stairs to the small file cabinet where I'd put the folder. When I returned downstairs, Roxie was on the phone.

I heard her give the information to another woman and waited. "Alright, I'll let her know."

I swallowed and looked at her, my eyes eager for information. "Well?"

"You can come in tonight. My boss is a little concerned about your family finding out what you're doing, however."

"You told her who my family was?" I asked, surprised at the invasion of my privacy.

"No, she ran your name and found out who you were in seconds. She doesn't just take anyone in, you know? She wants you to pick out a fake name, one that isn't associated with you at all. We tell most girls to do that if they want to, but with you, it has to be a fake name."

"Ah. Alright. I hadn't thought about it much; I just assumed I'd be protected, somehow."

Truth be told, I didn't really want my family to know what I had planned, but I also didn't care. My father would be disappointed, but he had his own life with my mother, and the two were busy traveling the world now that my brothers had taken over the family business. I probably wouldn't see them for another year, since they'd recently visited their estate in Charlotte.

"It's a huge thing, isn't it?" I asked softly and turned to look at her.

"You're going to sell your body, and maybe even your spirit and mind, to a man you don't know, Emily. It's more than huge; it's life-changing."

"Will you think it matters that I'm a virgin?" I'd left that part out, but she didn't look surprised.

"I think it will be a huge selling point, actually." She sighed the sigh of the experienced and then gave me a big smile. "I hope you get what you want from this, Emily."

"I do. I know I've never done, well, anything really, but I want this. I want it so very desperately."

"Just remember, you're protected there, no matter what. You can leave at any point, anytime you want to. There won't be any questions asked at all. You can just talk to the men, keep them company, or you can do more; it's all up to you."

"Thank you, Roxie. I really, I just…," I paused because I wasn't exactly sure what I wanted to say. "Thank you."

"I hope you're still thanking me the next morning," she said with a wry smile. "I want you to stick close to me the first night, alright? When I'm performing, I want you in the front row, where I can keep an eye on you. It's busy on Friday nights, so just keep your cool, remember who you are and why you're there, and stay in control, okay?"

"Yes, ma'am," I said with a wink. It was about to be go time.

## 6

# DYLAN

"What do you mean that one was taken off the market? It's perfect!" I stared at my phone as if the speaker on the other side could see the fury on my face.

"I'm sorry, Dylan, the city council have condemned the building for some reason. It's no longer for sale," Liz, the real estate agent, said from the other end of the line. "I will keep looking."

"Please do," I growled and cut the call. There wasn't anything else I could say, really, so I ended the call. It was infuriating.

"I know this is the work of Trent Thompson, I just know it is," I said to the person across from me. Freddy, the man who had shown me the ropes around town, and who knew all the right hands to shake. Obviously, Trent Thompson did too.

"It looks like he doesn't want the competition, that's for sure." Freddy stubbed out a cigar and sipped at his brandy.

"I don't get it. The place is crawling with resorts. It runs out of rooms on a regular basis during the summer, but he wants to block me?"

"Competition is fierce here, even if rooms do fill up. People want the newest, the latest, and they want a great experience. Something shiny and new at another hotel might draw the bookings away. Can't say that I blame the fella, to be honest. It's good strategy. Keep the new people out and you won't have to compete so hard."

"Fuck him," I growled and glared at Freddy. "Whose side are you on anyway?"

"Yours, my new friend, but I'm a realistic man. I'm not going to piss on your head and tell you it's raining. I'll tell you the facts of life, and the truth is Trent doesn't want you here. That's a fact that can't be changed."

I wondered for a moment if my past was the real culprit here. I'd been adopted, but not as a baby. I'd been old enough that the rumors that I'd killed my real parents had been plausible, if not likely. The rumors had persisted throughout my life. They'd included allegations of abuse, abuse so horrific that I'd snapped one day, killed my real parents, and ended up at an adoption agency. Like the questions about Jesse James, I didn't bother to sway people's opinion on the matter; it was pointless.

Something like that followed you, and I could even find mentions of it in online forums still. It wasn't talked about as much now, people soon had forgot about me, and more sensational killings eclipsed anything I might have allegedly done. Could that smidgen of history be the real reason Trent had worked so hard thus far to keep me out of the resort business here?

"I'd like to kick a few levels of sense into that man." Then I thought about it some more. "Actually, I think his brothers help run the business too. I'd like to break them all, show them they can't keep me out."

Freddy looked at me with skepticism, but he nodded. "I don't doubt you could do it too."

"I could, one way or another." I couldn't think of how though. The brothers had bought up a lot of the property I wanted, and they had now blocked the sale of the latest place I'd decided to make a bid on. How could I break them?

It wasn't a matter of money. I was a rich man, the properties I had on the west coast of America kept my bank balance eye-wateringly high, and I could buy almost any place I wanted to.

I really liked the atmosphere of Myrtle Beach, though, and I wanted to expand out this way as soon as possible. "Damn them all."

I clenched my fist and pounded on the table. "What you need to do is relax, son. Ole Freddy will find you something. I promise."

I nodded at the man, but I knew his kind of friendship came with a price I'd have to repay at some point. I didn't want to be beholden to him, and I wanted to find a place on my own. It didn't look like that would happen, however.

"Zoning laws suck here, by the way." There was a lot of property I could buy, develop into a resort, and make a killing off of, but zoning laws dictated what could be built where here, and they restricted a lot of land. Those laws were in place mainly because of hurricanes and were meant to help conserve the lush beaches in the area. I could understand that, but still.

"Can't get around those. Many have tried and failed." Freddy sat back in his seat at the bar we'd come to for drinks and a chat. We were in a dark corner, and the place was almost empty, so our conversation was private.

"I'll think of something." I sipped at the beer I'd ordered but hadn't touched yet. Liz had called the minute I sat down and dropped the latest bomb on me.

"I'm sure you will," Freddy said softly. "You heading over tonight?"

I knew what he meant. Elmo's. "Yeah, hopefully I'll

find something to take my mind off my troubles. I'm starting to get lonesome."

"What are the girls like in Kansas?" Freddy asked and tipped his empty glass at the bartender for another.

"The same as here. It's not all farms and windmills, you know? Our cities have some of the sweetest ladies you'll ever find, and a lot of them are the right kind, if you know what I mean."

We chuckled together, and Freddy said he'd have to travel out that way one day. "Come see me, if I'm there. I travel a lot for business, but I'll be glad to show you around if I'm there."

"That'd be great." Freddy nodded. The air around us was relaxed, and it stayed that way as more people came in. You want to head over to Elmo's?"

"Yeah, let's get out of here before it fills up too much. I hate crowds, and I know what it'll be like in there by ten."

"Wild." Freddy grinned as we paid our tab and left.

When I got to Elmo's, the parking lot had a few cars in it. Later, the party inside would be all but out of hand, but you wouldn't be able to tell outside. Most people came by taxi, or had a driver drop them off. That parking lot would never fill up.

I walked inside and found the music was already loud. It blared from the surround sound, and I saw

Hayley, another dancer, on the stage giving it her all. I had been in Myrtle Beach for a couple of weeks now, and I hadn't been laid since I got here. I was starting to get antsy, and the beauty on the stage caught my attention. She'd do for a night, maybe two.

Three was my limit, but I didn't always make that clear. I liked to keep my options open. I wasn't ready to settle down, and when I did, the woman would have to be more than special to keep my interest. I had women from all over the country at my feet, night and day, if I wanted them. I didn't need to be tied down to one just yet.

Although, if I found the woman who could handle my kind of play … the woman on stage caught my attention again. She'd shifted into a new routine, one that had her writhing along the floor as she pounded her fist to the industrial music. She had a hard edge, the vixen on the stage, and might be an interesting partner. She'd definitely bite back.

I forgot all about the Thompson family as the beauty dropped her top, and I was given a full display of large rosy nipples. The kind you could suck on and not get tired of. Sensitive nipples from the looks of them. The buds were tightly puckered, and the end stuck out at least half an inch. Yeah, the kind you could really get your teeth on.

I felt a rush of blood straight down to my pants and adjusted myself. The way she bent over, in that tiny, little, frilly blue skirt with white trim made even more blood flow, and I had to shift around in my chair a little more. That ass, demarcated with garters that ran down her thighs, made the vision she was even more tempting. A quick fuck, even against a wall in the hallway, would be worth it just to feel that lush ass against my thighs.

And in my palms. My hands twitched as I thought about it. She finished her set then, and a man came up to her. She melted into his arms, and I knew she was taken for the night, if not protected. Disappointment flooded through me, and I knew I'd lose it if I stayed there. Better to go into the dark confines below the building and find a dark spot to let my brain run free while I watched someone else partake in the game I wanted to play.

I'd had play partners before, quite often really, and I loved the thrill of it all. It wasn't always easy when you traveled the way I did, but every now and then I'd find someone who wanted to play as much as I did. I used the key Miss Maples had given to me and headed down the gas-lit hall. I knew where I was going and didn't have to think about it.

A new couple was there today. A woman, on her knees, her arms chained up over her head. She wore a mask, and it kept her long red hair from falling into her face. She wore a black PVC top that appeared to have been poured onto her torso and arms, and a pair of bright yellow panties. Something about those garish panties told me that her dom had put those panties on her.

I knew the pair inside couldn't see me or shadows of the people who walked by, but the man in there, in a mask that covered his entire head in black leather, looked in my direction. He moved to his sub; the small whip in his hands twitched along the woman's breasts, and she stirred. Her head had hung down as if in capitulation until the brush of the leather against her nipples.

She hissed in a breath, but the dom's face didn't turn back to his submissive. It stayed locked into place, on me. Could he see me, after all? I shifted around, shoved my hands down in the pocket of my trousers, and ignored the key card Miss Maples had given me a couple of nights ago. A grin spread over the man's face, a red slash revealed by the open zipper over the mouth.

The man moved, his head turned, and he reached out to the woman suddenly. With a hard yank, he twisted her nipple, and I saw her pained, surprised reaction in 3D. Her lips, painted a garish red that clashed with her hair, opened wide, her eyes were blindfolded so I couldn't see them, but I knew they'd be open beneath the black scarf tied behind her head.

Her nipples had gone tight, and the man stepped

back to admire his work. He tweaked the other one, and she seemed prepared now. That was sad, I decided. I'd liked her response. I saw the woman bite her lip and let it go, and I knew it was a tease.

This was all for the man in front of her. The man was fit, a giant compared to the tiny woman below him. She was slim, almost too small, but those nipples said she was all woman. Tucked against her feet perfectly, she had a round ass and slim thighs. Perfect for riding a giant.

I waited, but nothing more happened. They spoke to each other, although I couldn't hear exactly what was being said. I couldn't decide if I really wanted to watch their display or just find a quiet room to jerk off in before I headed back up. I could always head out, do it in my room, and have a lot more privacy.

I was about to turn away when the man took his cock in his hand and shoved it into the woman's mouth. I saw her body relax as if she'd been tense all along, while she waited for the one thing she craved. Now that she had it, she could relax. But not really.

I watched the display, my eyes attentive, as she took every inch of him. She was so small; I knew she shouldn't have been able to swallow that entire length, but she did and tried to go for more. Her slim hands clenched and unclenched as if she had her hands on him, but she didn't. She'd lost her control then.

I smiled, but my eyes narrowed on her. I watched the signs of her total capitulation, the way her body leaned into his, the way she eagerly swallowed every inch of him, and the way she wanted more. She had even started to squirm in place on the black square she sat on. I could see she was bare below the waist, totally bare, in all regards.

Every time he pulled away, slid out of her juicy mouth, the man's foot tapped at her knee and her legs would open slightly. More and more until I could see the evidence of how excited she was, even from where I stood. Blood surged in my cock, and I wanted to relieve the ache there, but I didn't want to be the sad fuck jerking off in a hallway.

The man hit a button, and the woman was lifted to her feet. There was a collar around her neck now that had her secured to a board. Inventive, I decided, but maybe a bit extreme for me. It did create a pretty picture, and the woman didn't seem upset about it.

She all but bounced on her feet as the man came up to her, lifted her legs, and wrapped them around his waist. She was at just the right height, and her body jolted as he'd thrust into her. Her hands were still working in their bindings, and I wondered if he'd taken the weight off of her shoulders. She'd be in too much pain otherwise.

He had her ass cradled in his hands, and though it

might look like he was out of control, he wasn't. The woman was safe and was soon screaming with pleasure as her body jerked against the board. That was what I wanted. Now, to find it. I headed back upstairs, eager to find my own playmate.

7

―――――

DYLAN

**S**ometimes people lived their entire lives without exploring their inner desires. They lived a quiet life, taking part in the same routine, every day, with small moments of joy found in that routine. They lived their lives blindly, they didn't look to the left or to the right, and they certainly didn't look at their own desires. They just lived until they died.

I wasn't that kind. I knew what I wanted. I'd explored it a variety of times. I'd opened minds and bodies to the ultimate experience that desire could bring to a human body. In the process, I'd examined my actions, the responses I felt toward that action, and replicated the ones that brought me the most pleasure. There was always room to grow, though, and I would try new things. With the right woman.

I'd settled into a chair at Elmo's and awaited the

promised siren that Roxie had enticed me with. I hadn't really planned to come to Elmo's tonight, the hunt was starting to wear on me, but she'd sent word through Freddy that I would want to make sure I was there for her set.

I didn't know a lot about the woman that Roxie had told me about, but I knew if the professional said I'd like her, then she had to be right. I waited as Roxie did a routine I'd seen before, but then the lights changed, and smoke began to fill the stage. Out of the smoke emerged a small, blonde siren. She was wrapped in nude satin, her full breasts were covered, her slim waist was exposed, as was her navel.

Her hair had been pulled back into a tight ponytail, and she wore a strip of the satin as a mask. The material on her body had been draped expertly and exposed a lot of skin, but it hid from the viewer's eyes the most intimate parts. I could see her there on the stage, her lips a shiny red that needed to be kissed, and firm thighs that needed to wrap around my waist. Oh yes, she would do.

Roxie took the woman by the hand, and I saw the newcomer's uncertainty. She stumbled but caught herself as Roxie led her to the pole. Roxie climbed as we all watched, and when she was up halfway, she took the woman's hand. Again, she was uncertain, but she was also brave. So, she could be led. She could fight her own fears to get what she wanted.

I ran a thumb across my jaw as I watched her, my concentration unbroken even when my finger moved to tap at my top lip while I watched. She wasn't as full in the hips as I'd normally like, but for a night, she might do.

I hummed as Roxie caressed the other blonde who stood with such regal presence, despite the fear that made her head turn as she sought to see who was in the audience. She held herself with pride; she wasn't cowed as some women were on their first night at Elmo's. She stood with her head held high and her body on display, now that she'd finally conquered the jitters that had shaken her at first.

Roxie's finger slowly brushed along the feminine line of the woman's jaw, an erotic move from a woman who hung upside down from a metal pole. They were a pair on the stage, and as an introduction it was seductive. The promise of innocence was enhanced by Roxie's overtly sexual pose. I liked the contrast.

I wanted to speak to her, to look into her eyes, so I waited patiently. Some of the women who came in wanted to strike out on their own and were completely independent, but I had a feeling Roxie would stay close to this one. She knew the woman, but she hadn't told me anything about the lady's personal life, other than the fact that she wanted to live a little.

Was she some preacher's daughter, out to take a little

shine off of her halo? Was that it? My eyebrows furrowed as the pair ended their performance and left the stage. Or, perhaps, some strictly raised Mr. Dark who wanted to find out if real life was better than the books she hid in? Or maybe a daddy's girl who wanted out from beneath his thumb? It didn't matter to me where the woman came from, but a woman who had been spoiled her entire life probably wouldn't like my world very much. I'd soon find out, I decided, and sat back in my chair. They'd make their way to me eventually, and I'd be ready for them.

They stopped at the table of a new member, and whatever he said made the princess blush and look away. But she still held her head regally, and I could tell she wasn't used to being spoken to so … familiarly. I felt my eyes narrow again and watched her with some amusement. It would be fun to break that regal air down, to watch her head go from poised and untouchable to a more, well, submissive air.

I felt my body respond to her, and I knew she was the one I wanted, most definitely wanted. She'd do quite well, and it wasn't just desperation for a playmate that led me to that conclusion. She was a prime candidate for my kind of play, and even if her manners and air said she was in control and always would be, I knew that what she actually needed was a firm hand and a red bottom.

She made her way to another table, Roxie at her side, and I could hear their conversation. She had the South Carolina Southern accent, but there was a refined edge to it. The syllables that were usually slurred came out a little more pronounced than you'd typically find in these parts, and the way she spoke screamed boarding school to me. That or she'd taken elocution lessons.

I took it all in, and what I found was a well-bred woman who probably came from money, and a lot of it, if the way she held herself apart from the club members meant anything. That wasn't nervousness, or even fear; it was confidence and training. She'd been taught to be a proper lady, and everyone who met her would always know it. From the way she spoke to the man with a polite but distant air, I knew she could hold a conversation with anyone and walk away without a hint of rudeness on her part. Capable too, then, I decided as Roxie led her to the bar.

The woman was given a glass of wine, and for a moment, they sat there quietly whispering to each other. Even in little more than scraps of cloth, the woman's pose said she was elegantly dressed and her attire wasn't anything unusual. She might as well have been wearing a suit with a scarf tucked around her neck for modesty's sake. Nothing touched her, but she wasn't an ice princess, far from it if that fire in her eyes meant anything. No, she was just a woman who knew what she wanted and hadn't found it yet.

She hadn't met me; she hadn't even looked in my direction. She just sat on that stool, as if at a garden party, and whispered to Roxie. Every now and then, she'd reach out and touch Roxie's arm. So, they were friends outside of this place, I knew. Where had Roxie met her? What would a woman like Roxie be doing at any kind of function this woman might go to? Or had they met in some bar somewhere?

It was all quite a mystery, and I wanted to find out what it all meant. If Roxie would stop playing games and just bring the woman over to me, we could get started. Roxie, however, was enjoying her little game of tease. I gathered as much when she cast a wink in my direction with a slight wave of her fingertips.

"Bitch," I whispered softly, but didn't mean it.

I knew Roxie was heavily invested in the place; otherwise, she wouldn't do so much of the work around here, and this was all part of an elaborate dance. From that little show on the stage, to the poised woman on that stool, it was all part of a plan Roxie had devised.

I'd strangle her if the tease of it all wasn't so fun.

A grim smile stretched over my face, and I sat back to wait a little while longer. Good things come to those who wait. I knew that well from my time here. The other hotels would be fine without me, for now, and I could spend a little more time out here. Most of the work I needed to do could be done from my computer in the small penthouse I'd rented today, and the rest could be done with phone calls.

In the past, my father had spent a lot of time on the road, going back and forth between hotels. I hadn't seen him a lot, and that was part of the reason he'd retired. He wanted to spend more time with his wife and play golf, so he'd handed over control of the hotels on the west coast of the country to me. I'd expanded the range when I bought hotels in New Orleans, Louisiana and one in Biloxi, Mississippi.

Taking our business to the east coast was proving almost impossible. There were other places to look, some down the coast and others up, but I really wanted to have one here in Myrtle Beach. I was patient, and I'd wait. Something would come along. Just like the princess on the stool over there.

There were rooms here, rooms we could claim permanently, for a price, or we could use them as our whims took us. The rooms that were claimed perma- nently could be decorated and kitted out however we liked. I'd take one of those rooms tonight, I decided as I looked her over. Give her a little taste of what was to come.

Roxie shifted off of her stool and took her friend's hand once again. I straightened in my chair as they came in my direction. I sat up straight and waited, my face impassive. Roxie's face was a mask of triumph as she finally brought the woman to me. They walked up to my table, in a darker corner of the bar, and stood there.

The woman looked at me, her eyes taking in the shape of my face, the bulge of my shoulders in the suit I wore, and the length of my fingers on the table. An arched brow told me she liked what she saw.

"Hello, Roxie. Who's this delicious little morsel you've brought to me?" I was much taller than the woman, and now that she was close, I could see that her body was perfection, even if her hips weren't very full. I would love every moment my hands were on her.

"This, my friend, is Stephanie. She's just joined us here at Elmo's, and I thought you'd like to meet her." Her voice was cool, but I could hear the amusement in it. She'd seen how I'd stared at Stephanie then.

If that was her real name. She didn't look like a Stephanie to me, not with those beautiful gray eyes, but I wouldn't judge.

"Hello, Stephanie." I turned my gaze to the woman and looked her over and over again.

"Hello, Mr. Dark." Her voice was barely above a husky whisper, and I felt a throb of desire.

"Mr. Dark?" I asked, confused, but willing to play along.

"Yes, you're tall, dark, and handsome. I think it suits you." The words came out on a flirtatious note.

I knew she'd be more than lovely at my feet, on her knees, with her head bent in submission. The image was so vivid in my head I faked a cough and pushed my hips under the table a little more.

"I can tell you my real name, if you'd prefer?" I offered, but she shook her head.

"No, Mr. Dark works, for now."

"For now. Indeed. Would you like to sit?" I held a chair out but didn't rise.

"I'll leave you two to get acquainted then. Freddy's just arrived, and I want to say hello." Roxie left us with a wink in my direction, and I turned to the delightful company I'd just been left with.

"Can I get you something?" I asked, and she nodded. She seemed to be a little nervous now that Roxie was gone, but she didn't panic.

"Rum and Coke, please." She twitched the material that was wrapped around her body and got settled in.

It only took a moment to get her a drink, and I came back with a confident smile. "Here you go, as requested."

"Thanks." She took a drink of it before she put the glass down. "Look, I'm new to this, and really nervous, so if I say something stupid…"

"It's fine," I interrupted I didn't want her to get upset and possibly run off. "You aren't the only girl to walk through those doors for the first time. Just relax. We all know why we're here, but there's no need to rush into anything."

I put my hand over hers and felt her warmth. I wanted her even more now that I'd heard her voice and seen those incredible eyes up close. She smiled, a little bashful now, but she leaned into me. She moved her bottom lip, and I knew she wanted to bite it; I wanted her to bite it, but she didn't. Instead, she looked away.

"It's nicer than I thought it would be," she said and turned back to me. "I expected something like you'd see in a movie."

"No, this isn't one of those places, and it's not a drug den. Drugs aren't allowed." I took a deep breath before I spoke again. "It kind of reminds me of the old gentlemen's clubs you can read about in novels set in the Victorian era. I've actually seen men reading newspapers and talking quietly here. It's, well, genteel, almost."

"Except for the stage," she pointed out, and I laughed.

"Except for the stage," I repeated with a low chuckle. "But it's not a bad place. Well, except for the dance club part on this floor. That can get pretty wild, but that's only open for special events."

"I see. And how does all of this work then?" She leaned forward, her elbows on the table as she picked up her glass to finish her drink.

"Roxie didn't tell you?" I was a little surprised at that.

Roxie normally took care of all of the new girls and told them the lay of the land.

"I know how it's supposed to happen, but real life is always different from what you expect, isn't it? I'm not sure how to proceed, exactly." Her eyes had been on mine as she spoke but had fallen down to her hands now that she was finished.

"Well, it's all up to you, Stephanie. If you should just so happen to find a man you like, you sit down, have a drink," I paused to tilt my scotch at her, "and talk about it."

"And what if the man doesn't want me?" she asked, a question in her eyes.

8

EMILY

"Then that man must be insane. Or blind."

I took a deep but steady breath as I let my eyes go back to him. He was right beside me, our legs almost pressed together, and excitement had rushed through my veins and a tightening of my skin.

I hadn't seen him from the stage, mainly because I'd been so nervous. I could barely see Roxie, much less anyone in the dark crowd, but I had when she'd subtlety whispered it to me at the bar. His face had been pointed down at his phone, but I could see it just fine. He had a gorgeous face, with high cheekbones, a strong nose, and eyes that were shaped beautifully. I couldn't tell the eye color yet, not from this distance, but I could tell they were light.

It was only when Roxie took me over to his seat that I figured out his eyes were gray, but a much lighter shade than my own. His almost looked like glass on a cloudy day, but clearer. Roxie had told me a little about him, that he was looking for a playmate and what that meant.

When she'd gone over the finer details, my eyes had glazed over, because I was still thinking about the term, playmate. Someone to have fun with, to play with, but in an adult way. And apparently, Mr. Dark's kink aligned with mine perfectly. If a virgin could have a kink.

I looked down at his hand over mine and moved my fingers to trace down the long length of his hand. Manicured nails, skin that had seen work but were smooth with no rough parts to tear at my skin. Hands that would engulf me, mold me, make me scream. If I let them.

I looked up into his eyes and saw a fierce gaze that didn't want to let me go. My breath caught in my chest as I looked into those eyes. They held promises and a certain kind of smugness that wasn't unattractive. On the contrary, it was the self-assurance that came along with the smug that made him even more attractive.

He didn't want the things he wanted to prove he was superior to a woman; he wanted them because he'd liked to be in control, to give pleasure, or to take it away at his whim. It was a power game, of course, but not a game of degradation.

"I would like to discuss the matter with you further,

but I promised Roxie I'd talk with her before I made my final decision. Do you mind?" I knew the mask was on and was aware of it as he looked at my face while I waited.

My fingers reached up to touch the edges, it was still in place. That would be one of my rules. The mask stayed on, or there was no deal.

"Not a problem. Take your time. I have all night." I didn't know male voices could be sultry until then. I took a big breath and stood.

It took everything in me to walk away from that table, and I waited until Roxie had dragged me into a dark corner to let the grin spread over my face. "He's perfect!"

"I know! But listen, I've heard he likes to play games. Games you might not be ready for, Emily."

"Stephanie," I corrected quickly, with a hiss, "I'm Stephanie here."

"Shit, I'm sorry. Of course, Stephanie." Her hand fell down to cup my shoulder. "I'm just worried he might be too … uh, experienced for you. That's all."

"No, he's exactly what I want. And dirty to boot, I bet. God, he's so perfect, Roxie!" When all you wanted was someone that fucking hot to make you scream their name as they fucked you, he was perfect.

"But, the other stuff, the uh, games…" She let the sentence trail off.

"I'm not the most experienced bird in the nest, I know that Roxie, but I know what those games are. I'm not afraid. It turns me on, actually." I'd never admitted that out loud, and I felt my cheeks flame even as I said them. She needed to know I'd survive this. "I have the rules you gave me, and the sense to know when I need help. I might not know the man, but I do know he's what I want."

"Alright then. If you're sure?" She looked me square in the eye and waited.

"I'm sure. Come on. Be happy for me." I pulled on her arm, and she smiled before she bent down to kiss my cheek.

"Be happy, Stephanie. That's all I want for you." She let me go then, and I walked back to Mr. Dark's table.

I wondered what his name was. Byron perhaps? Was his mother a poet who could see into the soul of her child to name him after such a man? Was she practical and named him John, perhaps? Or Biblical and named him something saintlier? Benedict, perhaps, or Moses?

It was hard to tell, but that was part of the fun. I wanted to spend a small amount of time with a man who would treat me well, who would open my eyes, and most importantly, get me off. I needed to be treated to whatever he had to offer; I needed Mr. Dark and his lovely games.

"Alright, do you want to discuss the practicalities?" I

knew he was as clean as me and would be checked regularly to make sure he stayed that way. House rules, and no fudging on health certificates.

"If that's how you want to do it, then we shall." He smiled as I sat, only I moved closer to him this time.

"I would like to have it out in the open." I worried I might be too forceful, not timid enough for a man who wanted a sub. But I wasn't his anything yet, and I'd do this the way I wanted to. It had to be that way. For now.

I'd tried a couple of adult forums, places that I'd never admit to being a member of, and had come across more than a few men who were clueless. Dick pics and demands that I get on my knees and suck their cocks as introductions just didn't seem … appropriate. Okay, you know how to treat a woman as a subhuman, good for you. That's not what I was after, not necessarily, and certainly not from those men. Subordination wasn't always meant to be demeaning. In many ways, it was meant to lift the sub up, to give them confidence, and the freedom to know they were safe to let go. They were safe to let the dominant one have the control.

Mr. Dark's eyes promised he knew all of that, far better than I did. Those eyes spoke of experience and confidence that I'd only learned to fake really well. Inside, I sometimes quaked with doubts, with misgivings about my worthiness for a life as good as my brothers had. I'd never accomplished things like they had; I'd barely even been able to finish my university degree, but not through my own faults. My responsibilities to my brothers and father had been overwhelming, and doing exams and papers in the midst of their chaos had never driven me over the edge.

I'd managed to get through it, though, I'd doubt any of them even realized I'd done it. We didn't celebrate my graduation, and I didn't make a huge fuss about it. They'd all been so … busy. Too busy to notice me.

I wasn't really upset about their lack of forethought when it came to me anymore. I was resigned to it. My birthday had been the final straw, though, even if they were apologetic about it now and had all sent me gifts. That wasn't what mattered. I didn't care about gifts; I cared that I mattered to someone. Even if it was only for a short while as we enjoyed the things life had to offer.

"I'd like to know what you expect, Stephanie." He flicked a hand, and the waitress brought us more drinks. I sipped at mine and studied his face.

"I expect to be treated with respect, Mr. Dark. I expect to be treated with dignity, cared for throughout our agreement, and I mean physically, not monetarily necessarily, and I expect you to retain control and not force your way through the agreed safe-word. If I use it, that's it—we're done."

"There can be no other way." He tapped at his

bottom lip with his index finger for a heartbeat that caught my attention, before he spoke again. "What else?"

"I expect to be pleasured, if I may be so blunt. I don't want a session of me sucking your dick, and then you walking off to leave me like my satisfaction doesn't matter." I couldn't believe the words coming out of my mouth, but I couldn't stop them either. I wanted to be clear on where I stood.

"Madam, I wouldn't dream of leaving you in such a state." He sat up and brought his face closer to mine. "I'm aware you may not be as experienced as some, but I can assure you, I know what I'm doing. And leaving you with anything other than my name on your lips, completely satiated, is the last thing I would ever do."

He actually said satiated. A man who knew what that word meant! My heart flipped in my chest. I put my hand over the fluttering organ and tried to talk it into calming down. Then the gist of what he said hit me. Totally satiated with his name on my lips. It conjured up all sorts of images of debauched pleasure that made heat wind from my stomach down between my thighs. I squeezed them together, but that only made it worse.

"Indeed. Then, we can move on to other subjects." I looked him in the eyes and waited. "What will you not do?"

"I don't do blood play. It's just not for me. No knives,

anything like that. If you want that, you'll have to find it somewhere else."

"I don't know what that is." Obviously, I hadn't gone as far down the rabbit hole as it was possible to go.

"Ah, I see. Some people like to be whipped until they bleed. Or cut. It's not something I participate in."

"No," I said and shook my head vigorously. "It doesn't sound like anything I'd like either."

"Good, then we're agreed on that subject. No blood."

"No vaginal penetration." I suddenly volunteered and looked down at the perfectly nude manicure on my own hands. "I, uh, I'd like to reserve that."

"Oh?" he asked and looked at me more intently. "Are you a virgin?"

Damn my cheeks! They burned, and I looked at him, but refused to feel ashamed. "I am. I'm not saving it for marriage or anything; I'm just … waiting."

"I see. No, that should be done correctly. I agree, Stephanie. Alright, no vaginal penetration then." His smile was a balm to my bruised ego, even if I could detect a hint of smug again. "I think I'll quite enjoy giving you lessons."

"Lessons?" I asked, not sure what he meant.

"You've never fucked a man before, right? Or sucked a dick. Or felt a man's tongue inside of you, I'd have to imagine."

"I, no. I haven't." My cheeks flamed all over again, but

I didn't back down. He'd been crude on purpose, to shock me and gauge my reaction.

"Then this will be lessons, on how to do all of those, how to take what you're given, properly."

I had a feeling this man would test my patience, far beyond anything I've ever experienced before. Even with my brothers, arrogant bastards that they all were, I'd never had to deal with a man who directed that arrogance at me. I wondered what he'd do, what he'd make me do, and anticipation began to make me nervous.

"What else, Stephanie?" he murmured, and I finished my drink.

"We have to start tonight." I gulped and looked at him, the glass now empty on the table.

"I stopped having any other plans for the night the minute I saw you on that stage."

"Really?" I smiled softly, pleased. "I'm glad you liked me."

"I do, indeed. I need to speak to our mutual friend, Roxie over there, and we'll have to sign some papers, but otherwise, I'm yours for the rest of the night, Stephanie. And three more if you'd like."

"Only three?" I asked, a little disappointed. Would that be enough?

"Only three," he repeated, his face a mask. "I'm not in this for a relationship or for long term commitments; if that's a problem…"

He allowed the words to trail off, and it hit me that I was about to let this man touch me in ways no other man had. He was a complete stranger, if a charming one, and I knew next to nothing about him. That made the whole thing even more naughty, and I smiled as my bravado came back to life.

I wasn't exactly on fire for the man, I'd barely just met him, but I felt a draw to him that I couldn't deny. "Three days would be satisfactory."

"Oh, it'll be far more than satisfactory, my dear," he murmured and ran his finger down my jaw. "You'll never forget them, I promise you that."

"I hope you can keep that promise, Mr. Dark. I really do." I watched his eyes as I issued the challenge and knew I was in for a lot more than I'd bargained for.

Those mysterious gray eyes went wide then narrowed down slightly before he looked away.

"Where's Roxie at? I think we need to start you on etiquette lessons, missy." The words were spoken softly, but with careful control.

Oh no, was I in trouble?

9

# DYLAN

*I* wanted to feel the burn of my hand over her bottom, I decided as the cheeky little monkey issued a challenge to me. She hoped I could keep my promise? I'd make sure she never forgot me, that was for sure.

But it wasn't violence that she'd remember me for. Oh no, now that I had a distraction for the next three days, I'd make sure little Miss Innocent knew every way to please a man, herself, and to be pleased. She wouldn't forget me, because I'd make her crave me.

I wasn't a cruel man, however, and I wanted it known up front that I didn't do relationships. It was too much stress and drama, both of which I didn't need. I had enough of that in my work life; I didn't need it in my play-time either. No, I'd found it much easier to be up front with my partners, that way there were no expectations.

I beckoned Roxie over once I caught her eye, and we went about the business end of the deal. The monetary sum Stephanie would be given as a token of appreciation, not for services rendered, was a bit high for the normal fee, but she was special. I'd already guessed she was a girl of breeding and taste, most likely educated at a boarding school with the manners and suave conversation skills that came with it. Even the way she tilted her head was practiced, controlled.

Everything about her was, though. Even now, she wanted control of the situation, to make demands, and I knew she hadn't quite grasped the situation. She was a sub, and in many respects, in control of me, but only in the way I responded to that. I needed to be sure she knew that.

"You do realize, once you sign your name to that document, you are to be at my beck and call? That you will, in essence, be mine?"

She took a deep breath, blinked for a moment, and then looked at me. "I have been in control my entire life, Mr. Dark. I've been at everyone's beck and call, but not a single person has given me anything in return. I want what you offer now. I'm fully aware of what it means, but I will get something out of it. I won't be left alone, in the dark, with nothing to show for it."

"I see." I waited for her to go on, but she didn't. I would enjoy breaking that control of hers. "Would you like another drink?"

She'd had two, but I'd offer a third if she needed it. I didn't want her drunk, but I did want her to be able to let her inhibitions go. Instead of answering me, she signed her name to the contract and looked at me directly.

"I'd like a bottle of water, a moment alone, and then I'd like to begin. If that's alright with you?"

Her left eye twitched, and I knew she was nervous, but she wouldn't give in to that state. Where should I begin with her, I'd wondered.

"That sounds acceptable. You will find me in the room assigned to us when you've finished."

"Thank you. I won't be long."

"Take your time." I left the bar the moment she did and found the room we'd been assigned. Our sort of play was a common enough theme that the establishment had set up a room that had been cleaned and sanitized, with everything we might need available. I walked in to find all was in order, that the toys we might need during our time together were new and in packaging to ensure sanitation, and that we had a fridge with snacks and a few drinks. I also went into a closet to the side of the room and found new pajamas available.

I decided to put on a black silk pair then went to the

bed to wait for Stephanie. The room had a table to one side with lubricants and massage oils in individual packs, as well as condoms. The rest of the room was meant for play. I'd explore it more later. For now, I wanted to get to know this pretty little angel and settle her in to what was to come.

I wouldn't rush her, but when the time came, I'd push her right over the edge. That was the moment a woman was at her most beautiful, when she finally snapped and gave in to her own desires, her own needs, and let her mind go.

I connected my phone to the Bluetooth speaker system, started a playlist, and adjusted the sound until the music was a soft background noise. I dimmed the lights until the large room was a place of mystery, full of shadows and dark places. I noticed a memory foam rug beneath a set of rings on the wall. I'd seen the shackles in the drawers, ready for use. Would Stephanie be ready for that tonight, or was this a girl who only wanted to play at being a sub?

From the way her eyes had flashed at me and the arch of her eyebrow on more than one occasion, I knew that Stephanie would be one of those women who would fight back. Even though she'd agreed to be a sub, she wouldn't be able to help herself, and then we'd have even more fun as I taught her to obey.

I was hard already at just the thought of it all and

tried to distract myself. I didn't normally react so quickly to a new conquest, but something was different about her. I brushed the thought off and let my head fall back against the bed. I'd waited weeks to find a new playmate and a property here, but I could wait a while longer.

She didn't want to be vaginally penetrated, but there were ways around that, ways to give us both pleasure without actual coitus. Such an ugly word, but appropriate in the situation. No, we didn't have to have penetrative sex to get each other off, and I'd delight in the myriad of ways we could accomplish that.

I'd noticed her fingers, long and delicate, the skin smooth without the tendons that turned so many feminine hands into claws. It was a huge turn-off for me, those hands. They reminded me of my adoptive mother, and well, it just freaked me out, so I avoided women with those kinds of hands. Stephanie's hands were beautiful, though, so no worries there.

I began to get impatient as I waited for her to join me in the room. Was she taking a shower or something? What was taking her so long? I could be a patient man, but I was impatient for more than one reason, and not just sex. I'd like to look at her a little more.

I wanted to see her body completely nude. I wanted to see her with her makeup smeared across her face, hands tied above her head and linked to a wall, as she begged me to make her come. And they were all things I'd do, if she allowed it.

There were a few more things we needed to talk about before we got started with this, and I waited for her to come in, a list in my head already. I knew what she didn't want, but what did she really want?

She was a virgin, but that didn't mean she had no idea about the world of sex. Plenty of virgins masturbated, watched or read pornography, or had vivid sexual fantasies. I needed to know what hers were, what limits she wanted to push, before I could take this further. I needed to have an idea of what her goal was.

We only had three days to reach those goals, so we had to be quick, but not too quick. Push too hard, at the wrong time, and you'd push your sub away. Do this with some control, with an understanding of the needs of the sub, and you'd have a sub for life.

The door opened, and she came in, now in a plain cotton gown that left her shoulders bare and ran down to the middle of her calves. Perfect innocence with a shy, but sexy appeal. Even the eyelet lace on the top concealed more than it revealed, but the effect was spectacular. Her hair was down, but her mask kept it pinned to her head.

I looked at her, in the gown that highlighted innocence but promised so much more hid beneath, and became hard again. The tilt of her head down, the lack of confidence now, the way she quietly came in and turned to shut the door, all spoke of nervousness, uncertainty, and I could smell submission in every move she made.

With her hands balled together in front of her, Stephanie came to me and waited at the side of the bed. "What do we do now, Mr. Dark?"

Sweetly asked, and my response was equally as sweet. A reassurance that all was well as I pulled her to sit beside me. "We'll do whatever you like, Stephanie. The night is yours."

She pulled her lip between her teeth, her hands still balled in her lap, and looked at the walls. "I'd like to know what all of those things are on the walls."

"They're for chaining and clamping a sub in place. I can have you on your knees as you wait patiently for me. Or standing up with your arms over your head. I could even have you in between. Up high on your knees, instead of low and relaxed. That makes *things easier.*" I emphasized the last two words and her eyes blink rapidly.

She'd caught that then. I knew she'd be responsive. I hadn't really touched her yet, and even now, her bottom resting against my thigh was the only place we'd touched. "There's water in the fridge there if you want it, and some snacks."

"I might have water, thank you." She moved to pull a

bottle out and took a sip as she sat on the far side of the bed. She put the bottle on the table beside of us and sighed. "I'm sorry. I don't really know what to do. Where to start."

"It's okay, Stephanie. Come here."

I held my hand out, and she came closer to me. With only a hint of roughness, just enough to make her breath shake, I pushed her head back and buried my hands in her hair. Her mouth opened, waited, and her eyes were full of apprehension, but also delight. I kissed her then, a rough kiss that held a gentle lover's touch. I forced her lips to open under mine and sucked her tongue into my mouth.

She moaned and leaned into me as she tried to repeat what I'd done, her hands in my hair, her mouth open to take mine. She was supposed to submit, though, not reciprocate. I pulled away, her face wet with my kiss. "Let me show you, Stephanie. Don't try to follow me. Just let me lead us."

She shook her head in acknowledgment, and I decided it was time to shred a boundary. If she couldn't see, she couldn't feel so safe. Her vulnerability would heighten her other senses, and she'd have to rely on me.

I pulled a long swatch of silk from the bedside table, and she looked at me confused. "But I already have a mask on."

"So you do, but this is not a mask, this is a blindfold.

You won't be able to see. I'll have to be your eyes for you."

"I understand." She waited, her hands folded submissively once again in her lap.

I moved behind her to put the blindfold on and ran my hand down her cheek. Her head followed the touch while she waited for more. "Now, tell me what you want, Stephanie. What you really want?"

"I want to lose myself," she said it quickly, as if she'd thought about it countless times already. "I want to forget the world exists and just feel."

"That's good. What else?" I sat behind her and waited for her to answer.

"I don't … I don't know what you mean." She turned her head in the direction she'd heard my voice and waited for an answer.

"How do you want to go about achieving that nirvana?" I said the words softly, to hypnotize her, to relax her. "Do you want me to spank you, to beat you into subspace? To the very edge of your limits?"

I let it all sink in, and the fact that she didn't turn away or take a breath of fear told me something. It wasn't out of the realm of possibility, though, it wasn't my favorite thing to do to a woman. If it got her off, though, that was what I'd give her.

I stroked a finger down the bare skin of her shoulder, down her arm, and around to cup the fullness of her breast. Her breath hitched then, and I knew I had her full attention. Her face turned toward mine, and I licked her mouth until she opened, a soft sigh the only sound she made.

"Or do you want me to drag you to the very edge of orgasm?" I clamped softly around a nipple I knew no man had ever touched before and squeezed it tightly. "Only to drag you back? To stop and leave you helpless?"

"That…," she breathed, her lips wet from my kiss. "I want to be yours, to only feel pleasure when you allow it, to be chastised when I do wrong."

"I think we'll take it slow tonight, Stephanie." That didn't mean she would be the same when I finished with her, but it would be safe. "Give me your hands."

I took another strip of silk from the drawer and tied her hands to the headboard. She'd be able to move them a little, but not far. She didn't protest; she just let herself fall to the pillows and followed my lead. Her hands were over her head now, and her breasts were a temptation I found hard to ignore, even in her gown.

I liked the idea of leaving it on, the contrast of it against her skin, the innocence of it I was about to besmirch. Like some duke of the regency era, I thought with a silent snicker. She was my virginal toy, and I was about to ravish her. Kind of. She had set a limit of no penetration. I'd see how long that lasted.

## 10

## EMILY

It was only when he had me tied to the bed that it all became real. Until that point, I'd taken it all in stride; I could back out, but this wasn't so bad. He'd promised to take me where I wanted to go in the large bedroom with walls decorated with hooks. He'd promised he'd stop if I said red, and he'd slow down if I said yellow. It was all safe, legit, and cool.

Until he tied me down. That was when I almost panicked and almost screamed red. It was because of the blindfold. I didn't know if he was looking at me, if he was sending a text; he could be doing anything. And there was nothing I could do about it. I told myself to relax. I tried to talk myself down, but I couldn't. I needed to sit up. I needed another minute.

Mr. Dark, as I'd insisted he not tell me his name, placed a hand on the outside of my hip, and calm washed over me suddenly. "It's alright, Stephanie. I know you want to stop, but just give it a moment. Relax into it. It's become real, suddenly, and a little scary, but the fear will pass."

He was right, or maybe it was that intimate touch, not sexual, just intimate, against my hip. Either way, calm came over me, and I was able to focus again. "Are you claustrophobic?"

"No, it was just a moment. It's gone now. You were right. Thank you." I licked my dry lips and wondered if I should call him master. I thought that might be a line too far into cliché land, but if he wanted me to…

"Good. Now. I'm going to touch you, Stephanie, and I want you to lie very still; do you understand? I don't want you to move or wiggle around, just lie very still." His body slid down mine, until his face was around my hips.

I waited, breath held, until he told me to breathe with a soft laugh that relaxed me. I stayed there like that and concentrated on not moving a muscle. He rested his head against my hip and let me get used to that before his hand moved to my knee. He pushed my knees apart until my thighs began to spread. His finger spun tight circles around the inside of each knee, until he moved up a little.

Softly, slowly, he circled his way up my thighs, until his hand found the edge of my panties. They were nude colored, and I'd spent a long time in the bathroom as I wavered over whether to leave them off or on. I'd wished I'd taken them off now.

My excitement grew within me as he circled his way up my silky, smooth thighs. What was an invasive touch at first had now become exciting, and the apprehension flared into a need to move, to urge him to do more. I wanted to groan in disbelief when his fingers moved to the bare space of my hip, until his fingers met resistance again. I'd wanted him to tear the panties away, to slide beneath them; whatever it took to make it bearable.

He pushed the nightgown up then and explored the edge of the panties, his fingers a skim on my stomach. I breathed through it all, but I was also concentrating hard on not moving. Don't move, I repeated in my head, even though I wanted to. Don't move, or he'll stop and make the most incredible thing you've ever felt stop. Don't move, or he won't make you feel even more.

I didn't want it to end, especially when his right hand moved up my left side, a swift movement that brought him to my ribcage, just below my breasts. I held my breath again but let it out when his finger traced the bottom curve of the skin that had never seen sunlight. At least, not outside it hadn't. No man had ever touched me, not there, and it was a moment of discovery for me. I liked to be touched there.

"Tell me what you want, Stephanie," he whispered against my hip.

"I want you to touch me." Simple enough, right?

"Where?" he asked, a hint of impatience this time.

"There." His finger had stopped its course up my breast, stilled now on the inside curve, just across from my nipple, tighter than it had ever been before.

"Where there?" No impatience this time, just resignation. I didn't like that disappointment there, and I wanted to make it go away. He was supposed to be pleased with me; I was supposed to please him, but I'd failed already.

"On my nipple. Please. You're the only man who's ever touched me there, and it feels so good when you do."

"Who could turn down such a pretty request?" His finger slid over my skin, pushed the gown up around my neck, until I was bare. His fingers closed over the sensitive skin, and I let out a breath of air when his fingers closed over it.

It was exquisite, not painful, but it made me want to move. I moaned softly as his finger squeezed tighter, and my hips twitched.

"Don't move, Stephanie, or I'll stop." His lips, against my other hip, were a soft brush against my skin. His breath blew across the exposed skin of my hip.

I didn't want to be disappointed in either of us when

this was done, and if he would hold up his end of the deal, I'd try my best. "Yes, sir."

"Mmm, a nice choice, Steph." I felt a glow of pleasure for his praise. "It's not necessary, but freely given it is a pleasure."

I closed my eyes, happy that I'd done something right. I didn't want to displease him, at all, not when his fingers felt so nice.

His face moved over the thin, silky fabric of my panties, until his mouth was just over my sex, his chin rested between my thighs, and I held my breath all over again.

"You know, if you spend the entire night holding your breath, you won't enjoy this."

I wanted to protest, to tell him I would, but I couldn't concentrate on not moving and breathe properly when he teased me like that. Was he going to touch me down there? I'd seen it on videos, but was it really good? Did men really like it?

I mean, there was a smell there, not unpleasant, but different. Would he like the way I smelled? Tasted? He was experienced, so I was sure he knew the details of a woman's body, but would I be right in that department?

His fingers squeezed even tighter, almost painful, just as he opened his mouth over my panties. His teeth found that spot there, the one that ached the most, and I felt a buzz in my ears. His other hand came up to press his thumb there, and the buzz grew in intensity. "There, touch me there, please."

It entered my head that I'd just begged a virtual stranger to touch my private parts, but I didn't care. I wanted to know what it felt like when another human being touched me there, and he was about to show me. Even if it was through my panties. It still felt heavenly.

"Very good, Steph." His fingers hooked into the panties for a moment, long enough for his tongue to lick across the spot, and my hips moved. "But that's not."

"Don't stop," I begged, but he let the fabric go and replaced his tongue with his thumb.

"Lesson one. Don't move."

"But it felt...,"

"No, I told you not to move, and you did. No protests. Just take your punishment, my dear." His thumb worked the spot, just the right pressure, just the right pace, and I wanted more. "You do taste nice, though, so later, when you've earned it, I'll taste your pussy again."

"Ohhh..." I breathed out, and my hips dipped into the bed at his naughty words. "That would be wonderful, sir."

"Indeed, it would be wonderful, Steph." He shifted around to sit beside me then moved me carefully until I was on my stomach. I could go to my knees once he fed more cloth through the bars of the headboard, and he positioned me to prop up on my elbows. "Don't move, Steph. Stay like this."

"Yes, sir," I responded, but I felt exposed, vulnerable. Then I remembered, I didn't have to feel like that with him. I was supposed to give him those things. I let my head rest on the bed, still blindfolded, and waited.

His hand explored my bottom; his fingers dipped along the edges but didn't invade. "Now, if you're very good and don't move, Steph, I'll take these off of you and let you feel my tongue on you. But if you move, they stay on, and it's only my fingers you'll feel. Over the panties."

"Yes, sir," I repeated, and I knew I was screwed. How could I stay still like this?

"I can smell you through your panties, Steph, feel how wet you are. My cock would slide into you so well right now. I bet it wouldn't even hurt a little bit, despite your virginity." His fingers slid down my bottom, along the edge of leg, until he found the wet center he so eloquently spoke of. "I've not had a virgin for a long time. I have to admit, it is appealing to know you've never had a man's fingers on your clit before, or sliding through your wet folds."

"Is it, sir?" I could barely breathe as I waited for his touch, but he'd stopped, just hovered over the round fullness between my thighs, the mound that his fingers would soon be in, if I was a good girl.

"It is, Steph. So sweet to know you're untouched."

His fingers *pressed* into me then, a soft pressure, but enough to tease that ache above his fingers. They spread out then as I moaned softly, until he pressed into the spot.

His fingers danced on me until I couldn't breathe, and my hips wanted to move. I had to concentrate so hard on that, to not move, while he made me want to writhe with abandon. It was so unfair, but I did my best.

Until his other hand dipped under me to tease a nipple. My hips twitched, and his hand stopped, but then pulled my panties up tight, until the front pressed against my clit. Something had built inside of me, a pressure that was about to go off when he did that, and I gave a cry of protest. "Don't move, Steph."

"But…,"

"No. Do not move." He punctuated it by pulling the panties tighter. That only made the ache worse. "Concentrate, breathe."

"I just want to come." I'd never said that before, not out loud.

"I know you do. But you can come when I say you can, Steph, not before." This time his punctuation was a slap right against my center, and fuck, it felt so good. "Oh!"

"More?" he asked, his voice on alert.

"I liked that, sir. May I have another?" I didn't care what I sounded like; I wanted to feel that again.

His slap against my private was more forceful this time, mainly his fingers, but it felt so good I could barely control myself. I examined it as he waited for my response, surprised at myself. I wanted to try this out, but I wasn't sure I totally understood it. I'd never been the kind who thought hitting was something a man should do to a woman, but in this instance? It made me melt.

"Another..." I didn't realize my plea was a demand until I'd said, but he didn't point it out either.

This time, his palm caught my mound, his fingers the back of my thigh. Not as good, but nice. "I prefer your fingers."

"Good girl, don't be afraid to say what you like. To ask for it. But no more demands." He smacked my folds harder, and it didn't feel like punishment at all. It felt like heaven.

I wanted to squirm like a happy puppy, but I kept myself still. My hands were knotted on the white, lightly scented duvet that smelled clean and fresh, but I didn't move. "More, please, sir. Please, make me come."

"Very good, Steph, very good." His other hand still had my panties in a bunch, and I groaned when his tongue found my clit.

"Fuck..." I couldn't help it, the word came out as his tongue licked over me just before his lips sucked the small nub with a force I couldn't fight against.

His fingers didn't stop moving, and one hand went back to a nipple, while the other hand did something else. He slid it along my nether lips until he could clamp them between his fingers. He pressed them into the folds, and I wanted to squirm at it all.

I wanted to beg him to fuck me, but I was saving that. For a special moment, for the point when I knew it was completely right, and not just a newly discovered need. I imagined him behind me, pounding into me, a thick cock between my slick pink skin, and the world exploded.

"Sir…" I cried out into the air, my hips pushed down into his fingers, and my back arched, but I didn't twitch, not yet. I fought to remain still, to be a good girl, but I'd lost the moment the orgasm struck me.

"You may move now, Steph." He released me, and I cried out again, while my hips moved against his hand, and my back arched tighter. "Feel it Steph, let it take you away."

"I, oh fuck, I can't…"

"You can let go. You can move. You can do whatever you want." Then his fingers pressed harder, insistently, until the world spun away again, into this explosion of muscles and pleasure that I couldn't say no to.

In that instant, I was an addict who never wanted their high to end. No wonder people sought it out, and this was only my first orgasm with another person involved. What would sex be like? Could it beat this?

His tongue swiped at me, until it became unbearable, but he wouldn't move away. His hand planted down in the center of my back, and I knew this was a new lesson. Let him take control, or we'd end this.

Who could say no to a good tongue-lashing?

## 11

## DYLAN

I was enthralled by Stephanie. Despite her inexperience, she maintained her control very well, and I knew this must have been a daily occurrence for her. Not the sexy part, that was definitely new, but the maintain control part wasn't. My girl was very familiar with that.

I was impressed, as I had been from the moment I saw her. She gave in easily to her desire to be pleased, but she tempered that with a stringent control. I had the delightful job of breaking that control, though I asked for it. Perhaps confusing to some, but if you've never seen someone like Stephanie let go of that stranglehold on their control then you wouldn't understand. It was a paradox, but one that made sense to me.

"Roll over, sweetheart." I ran a tender hand down her back, to soothe her and let her know she was safe.

"Thank you," she said, out of breath but happy.

"It was my pleasure, Stephanie. Drink some of your water. You need to hydrate." It was consideration more than anything. Her skin had a light sheen from her exertions, and she needed to replace the moisture she'd lost.

She reached for her bottle of water and took several long swallows. I watched her throat work and knew where we were headed next. When she was ready.

I didn't just want her on her knees to suck me off and leave, as she'd said, but the image of her in that position did make me throb, and I wanted it.

I'd let her rest, then I'd work her up to it.

I watched her for a while, until her chest was calm and her eyes opened. I sat on the edge of the bed, patiently waiting for her to be aware once again. When it was clear she'd calmed from her exertions, I moved down to place a hand to each side of her head. Her arms came up to wrap around my neck, the silk a soft tickle against my ear, and she held me close as our bodies melted together. Her warm softness blended with mine everywhere our bodies touched, and I felt a burning need throb through my cock. She opened her mouth to ask for more, to say she was tired? I didn't know because I bent down to lick at her lips before I kissed her for a long moment. She nipped at mine in return and began to explore my mouth, confident in herself now, ready to explore me, to pleasure me. It was a relief when she smiled seductively at me. I allowed her the moment, the touches, then slid down beside her so she could explore more easily.

"Is it wrong to do this? Should I wait for you to order me to do something?" Stephanie pulled away to ask.

"No, not at all," I said lazily, and I looked at her with eyes that smoldered with desire. I'd given that look to more than one woman and watched her inhibitions melt, so I knew it worked.

"Thank you, sir." She boldly bent to kiss my neck, and her lips slid along my shoulder, pushing black silk out of the way.

She undid the buttons slowly, her lips following along as she did so. She bared my chest, smooth and hard, with a few tattoos I no longer paid any attention to. One was a skull that I'd had done when I was a teenager and full of anger. Another, a slash down my right side, was a black panther stretched out along the slim expanse. Yet another, on my left pec, was a revolver, another stupid choice of a teenager. I'd have them covered when I could be bothered.

Stephanie didn't linger over them. She wanted to feel the rest of me too much and continued to explore me with her hands. I hissed in a breath as her hands smoothed over my chest and down to the edge of my pajama bottoms.

"Slow down, Steph. Learn my body first." I guided

her hand up to my abdomen, where more hard lines met her fingertips. "We have a long night ahead of us; don't get in too much of a rush."

She looked as if she wanted to protest, so I moved. I straddled her to kiss her again, my forearms on each side of her head so that my fingers could tease at her forehead. Her lips were used to mine now, and she welcomed my tongue by opening her mouth to my exploration. I took my time, but I reminded her of what I needed when I pressed my hips into her soft stomach.

Stephanie pushed into me and made a sound in the back of her throat. "Was that a protest?"

"I want to feel you pressed into me," she said without hesitation. My kitten was already turning into a she-lion.

I nudged her legs apart and gave her what she asked for. I could feel her wet heat through the thin material of the pants, and I sighed deeply as I kissed the spot beneath her ear. "You're so hot, Stephanie. So wet for me."

Her head moved, lost, until she found my neck and kissed it. I brought her hands up over her head and shortened her reach.

A sound of protest again, and I ran a finger down her neck, to the tight peak on her left breast. "Only for a little while, my darling. Then you can touch me again." I knew her nightgown was bunched up at her hips, her panties still exposed but so wet from her excitement. I would look, but I was busy, my lips on hers.

She kissed me in a way that spoke of need now, not just curiosity. She knew for certain what she could attain and wanted it again. She lay exposed to me, but I didn't look; I was too captivated with her mouth still.

"Are you going to fuck me?" she asked me when I pulled back to give her room to breathe.

"You put it in the contract, Stephanie. I'm sorry, I can't." That contract meant very little legally, and we could break whatever rule we'd put in place, if we decided to do that together, but I wanted to tease her a little more.

"Oh." It was a sad little 'oh', and I had to hide a smile.

Her desire was growing, I could feel it in the heat she encased me in between her thighs, and I'd barely even touched her. Memories must be flashing through her mind.

I felt her take a shaky breath as my lips explored her hairline, and she pulled her head away. I allowed her the insubordination when I felt her lips just below my ear, and then her tongue darted out to taste my skin. She wanted to explore me again.

"Are you sure you can't fuck me?" Her question came out soft, almost afraid. Did she think her question would break the spell? Make me leave her? I didn't know, but I wasn't about to leave, not with my cock so hard for her.

"I can't, Stephanie. Not now. You'll have to make do with what's in the contract."

"Alright," she said and sighed, her head back down on the pillow again. "That was stupid of me. I didn't realize how good you were. Roxie told me you had a reputation as someone hard to please, but who could get the job done. I didn't know how right she was."

"I'm not sure what the ladies around here might have to say, but I know what I like. And how to please a woman." My fingers brushed down her neck then back up to tease her.

I decided then to give her another round of what she had been missing in her life. I could wait a little while longer. She was all but breathless as my lips danced slowly over her neck to a spot toward the back that I wanted to explore. She held her breath as I kissed the spot until I nipped at it with my teeth and began to suck. The air exploded from her lungs, and her knees came up to clamp me between her thighs.

"Sir!" Her cry was a tease, a whisper that made me throb all over again. Yes, it said, I like that spot.

I sucked at it and ground into her heat, and I almost chuckled when I heard the silk rasp along the rails of the headboard. She wanted to move, but her body was hampered. It must have been hitting home that I could do anything I wanted to her now, that she'd beg me to do it, if only she knew exactly what it was she wanted.

I was a stranger to her, a man she'd met only hours before, but already I'd done far more than any other man had ever done. I'd shown her passion, the fulfillment of that passion, and how to want a man all over again when she thought she was done. I groaned with pleasure when she pushed herself into me, into the hardness of my cock, into the sucking of my lips on her neck, and into the cup of my palm where one hand now cupped her breast. I tweaked her nipple, and she almost twitched away from me then. I pushed the top of her gown down, just enough to expose a pretty pink nipple, rosy with desire now that it was a tight bud. I scraped my tongue over it and drank in the sound of her groan with growing excitement.

"Sir, please. Don't stop." She wanted more, and I was more than willing to give it to her.

Her skin was silky soft, scented gently with orange blossoms. She was pale, which told me she didn't often go out in the sun. She wasn't one for tanning beds, either, and I had to admit, that look had started to turn me off quite a few years ago. I breathed over the bud for a moment, scraped at it with my smooth chin, and finally, when her hips started to buck against mine, I took her nipple into my mouth and sucked at it with tight pressure. Her legs wrapped tightly around my hips, and I pushed myself down into her as a pang of pleasure tore through me.

She tasted so good, she felt so good, and for a moment my control slipped as I sucked at her nipple with glee. I felt her hands dance along my body, and I knew those touches were meant to urge me into action, into doing what she'd asked me not to do.

She pushed at the soft fabric of my pants, but I grabbed at her hand to make her stop. She gave a growl of frustration when I held her hand still and would not budge.

"You said you didn't want me to fuck you, Steph. Stop it." I was teasing us both now. I'd fuck her if I damned well felt like it, now that I knew she wanted it, but it was so fun to tell her no, to make her regret her own demands.

"But, Mr. Dark." She breathed the words, and I could hear her desperation.

"No. You said no. You get this and nothing else."

I pressed my fingers between us to the slip of her underwear and found her clit quickly. "You can have my fingers *on* you, but not inside of you. You can even feel this."

I paused to pull away, expose my cock, and slide it along her slit before I let the fabric go and spoke again. "But you can't feel it inside of you."

My fingers went back to her clit and pressed into her, just right. "This is all you get, princess."

I slid two fingers down her folds and let my palm take over on her clit. She thrust up to meet the pressure, her body on fire all over again.

I pressed the length of my fingers against her and ground my palm down in time to the suction of my lips on her nipple. I let her move this time, and my enjoyment of her sensual slither almost undid me, but I held on. I pressed and sucked until I felt her go tense, and her back arched. A sound tore from her throat, and I held on to her, lost in her beauty as she came again.

She didn't just lay there this time, though; she moved against her bonds. "Let me please you. Please, sir, let me get you off."

"And where did you learn such language, my pretty?" I asked, but I didn't care. I was too busy releasing her hands and tying them in front of her to care.

"I watched videos, sir, a lot of them." I heard her say, eager now to feel relief from the pressure in my cock and balls.

I stood and pulled at her until she moved down to her knees. I'd wanted it, pictured it, and now, I had to have it. "Well, then you know what I want, don't you?"

"I admit, sir, I thought this was degrading in those videos, but I want it. I want your cock in my mouth."

She moved her head around, as if she sought the member out.

"This you mean?" I took my cock in my hand and let it slap gently at the right side of her face. She didn't answer verbally. Instead, she took my cock between her lips eagerly, and I nearly came right then.

Her technique was naïve, but she caught on when I held my hand to her head. She moved on me at first, her hands between us to grip at my shaft. When she moved her hands and started to take more of me in her mouth, when she started to suck instead of just moving up and down, I began to thrust my hips. I'd lost my control then, and she might not realize it yet, but my sub was the master in that moment.

"Stephanie…" I ground out her name, my jaw clenched as I reached for that moment. I needed to come. I'd pleasured her, fantasized about her, and now, I needed relief. "Make me come, baby, make me come."

Her sweet lips, so unpracticed but still so good, gripped at my cock, and when she purred in happiness, I felt my knees go weak. Orgasm hit me, and she didn't pull away even when I tried to pull at her face. She swallowed every drop of me, like a good girl, and I let her have her way.

## 12

## EMILY

The soft buzz of my phone was an insistent noise I couldn't ignore any longer, and I opened my eyes. He was asleep behind me, and I smiled, secretly pleased that he'd stayed with me through the night. I reached for my phone, pushed the mask away, and slid from the bed. I headed to the bathroom and looked at the messages that had kept my phone buzzing for so long.

Trent wanted me to watch the kids; their sitter was sick. Mason wanted me to come watch his too, because they hadn't found a sitter yet. Kevin wanted me to know that Ember was going on tour again, and would take her daughter with her. Well, two out of three wasn't bad.

I found the nightgown from the night before and slipped from the room after I wrote a note on the pad on the bedside table.

*Thank you for a wonderful night. Let Roxie know when you want night number two. I look forward to it. -S*

I didn't know what else to say, so I left it at that and went to the room where my clothes had been left for me. I was in a rush to get home to my huge bathtub and memories of the night before. I didn't think he'd be the kind for morning-afters, so I'd left him to it.

My virginity was intact, but barely, I thought with a smile. He hadn't even taken my clothes off, yet he'd managed to get me off in so many ways. For a minute, I almost turned the car around and went back. We hadn't agreed to three days straight, or three off and on; either way, I didn't have a toothbrush there, but if he wanted me to come back, I would. After I'd had a bath and cleaned up first.

I noticed light bruises on my neck when I glanced in the mirror after I took my clothes off. I smiled, happy because I knew how they got there. They weren't from violence, far from it.

That made me hum as I slid into the bath filled with hot water and bubbles. Violence wasn't something I was normally attracted to. But when I thought about how he'd softly slapped me down there with care to hit just the right spot, with sweet care, I felt desire burn through me. I imagined how it would feel to have that same swift slap on my bottom and squirmed in the tub.

"God, it's just too much," I said out loud to nobody. That made me laugh, and I submerged myself.

"But what if he wants some of that other kind? Well, no, he said he didn't like blood, and those videos I've seen of women with dark purple bruises were surely something he steers clear of?" I remembered how he'd touched me with gentle pressure, always gentle.

No, Mr. Dark was a dominant, I couldn't doubt that, but he wasn't violent. Some light slaps, a growl or two, maybe more if we really got into it, but I didn't think he'd do anything that would really hurt me. And it was only for three days, so we didn't have very long to delve down the rabbit hole, did we?

I got a text from Roxie a few hours later, so I called her. "Hey, girl, how are you?"

"I'm good. More importantly, how are you?" She sounded cautious, like she was walking on eggshells.

"I'm really good. Fabulous, in fact." I laughed and went to the window by the kitchen sink to look out at the world coming to life. "It's a beautiful Saturday morning, and all is well."

"Did you … I mean, did he stay within the terms?" I couldn't believe she was being so bashful, but I appreciated the fact that she was being considerate of my sensibilities.

"You mean did he fuck me? No, it's part of the contract. But I did ask him to." I sighed then, a little sad but also pleased. He was a man of his word, and it also made it a little hot. I had wanted it, but he wouldn't give it to me.

"Well, what the hell? Did you, you know? At all?" Still cautious, respectful.

"Get off?" I asked bluntly, and I wanted to laugh when she giggled. We were grown women who could barely talk about sex. It was almost funny.

"Yes! Did you?" Excitement entered her voice now, and I wanted to jump up and down like a schoolgirl.

"So many times!" I said with a lot of feeling. "It was so good, Roxie. I can't believe I've missed out on that for so long now!"

"Well, you don't have to do without it anymore. He has an appointment tonight, but he's asked when you'll be free again." Roxie sounded like she was pleased with herself, and I couldn't help but smile.

"Thank you for this. I was hoping to see him tonight, but if he's busy, I can wait. Um, will he call you when he's ready?" I didn't know how this worked. We hadn't exchanged contact details, and I didn't want to look desperate.

"Yeah, he'll call me. Look, go relax, if you aren't already, and have an easy day. Sex can take a lot out of you, so get some peace for a little while." Roxie sounded like she wanted to say more, but someone called out that she was needed, and we hung up after a short goodbye.

I almost wished I'd stayed now. I didn't know he had an appointment tonight or I would have. Another chance to get him to try to break the rules. I was quickly learning that this wasn't a situation where I had no control. I had all of it, to a degree.

I felt empowered, far more than I'd ever been before, and as if I was the one who held all the reins. Mr. Dark might lead us both, he might have the final say, but it was what I did, how I acted, and what I said that really mattered.

It had been a night of discovery and wonder. Maybe that was cliché, but it was true. I'd learned so much from him, and I wanted to have it all over again.

I did wish I'd picked something closer to my real name, though. It had been odd to hear him call me Stephanie. Maybe I should have picked Emma, or something like that, something that wouldn't sound so … different. I'd decided on Stephanie so he wouldn't know my real name. I wasn't ashamed of what I'd done, but I didn't want to bring shame to my family.

If people found out that Emily Thompson was working at a gentlemen's club and had sold her evenings to a stranger, then life as we knew it would be over. We'd be shunned from the circles that had always looked to us for leadership. I'd be laughed at, mocked, and probably kicked out of every charity I took part in.

Roxie hadn't been, but she came into the one we

worked together on with her background in the open. I was supposed to marry someone nice and quiet, deferential to my brothers and father, who would give me babies to carry on the Thompson traditions, even if they weren't Thompsons by name.

Anger surged through me for a moment. I hated my family sometimes. Not necessarily the people, but what we stood for, the constraints placed upon us by our name. I'd heard, "you're a Thompson, act like it" so many times while I'd been growing up that I didn't know what it was like to not act like a Thompson. Except, I never really had.

I was what the Thompson males wanted me to be. But now, with Mr. Dark, I could be exactly what I wanted to be, while at the same time, I could still be what my nature made me ... a sub. I wondered then if Stephanie had become a new persona for me. She was almost real, almost something ... other.

She took what she wanted, now that she knew what it was, and she'd sat there on her knees to suck that delicious dick like she'd been born to do it. I knew I was no expert, but he'd got off, and that was all the skill I'd needed, right? Well, to make it nice would take practice, but he'd reached the goal point anyway.

I didn't feel bad about it. It felt erotically dirty actually, naughty, to think about the memory. I'd loved it when his tongue had been on me. I'd loved how he'd touched me, but I'd adored it when he put me on my knees. I might have said that wasn't all I wanted to do, but he'd noticed that I'd said it and realized I'd wanted my own pleasure, but I really did want to do that with a man. And he'd given me that experience.

I wondered how many women knew you could get off without being naked? My cheeks turned red, but I grinned anyway. He'd touched me with such strong, sure hands, even a little roughly a few times, and I'd loved it.

I guess we'd have to explore later, find out what it was I really liked. I kind of wanted him to try a whip on me, but not like, make me scream from pain and fear whip me. A nice sensual sting of pain.

I wanted more than that. I wanted to be a mess of begging need for relief, but I knew that would take time, and I didn't think a few hours in the night was enough. Like my virginity, the point where we could engage in a long night of trusting BDSM was for the future. If he'd wanted one.

He'd said he was a three-day kind of man, though. I wondered if I'd give him my virginity then. He'd be gone after that, and I'd go back to my normal life, to pretend I was a daddy's girl still. Would I want to give that to him if he was only going to leave me?

I wasn't sure, even if I'd been certain last night. I was really impressed that he'd told me no, but it was an example of supreme control that he had. Not many men would have been able to say no when a woman was begging for their dick, I thought with a giggle.

"Fuucccck!" I droned out. "What am I going to do all day?"

I had nothing to do, at all, and so I decided to head out to the Boardwalk and see what was happening out there. I soon found myself lost in a horde of tourists, all of them trying to take in the sights. I hated vacations like that, where you had to cram everything into two days, and you'd go home exhausted.

That was why I hadn't gone to Italy yet, even though I'd wanted to. I wanted to go when I had months to travel around, to slowly take in the sights and scenery. My family hadn't given me that time. Even now, two of my brothers still didn't quite get that I wasn't the family doormat anymore.

Luckily, my parents had left me alone, but they were still away. That might change when they came home. I'd hoped not, it was hard enough to be upset with my brothers. I heard my phone buzz, saw it was Mason again, and turned my phone off. They had to learn to respect that I wasn't going to be at their beck and call anymore.

I'd miss a call from Roxie, if I left the phone off, but I knew she'd be getting ready to perform and then spend her evening with Freddy. He'd been cuter than I'd thought he'd be, and I could see why she liked him now. The way his huge hand had wrapped around her bottom had made something like jealousy prick between my shoulders. I wanted that one day, that intimacy, that possessiveness that let you both be comfortable with such an intimate touch as an open declaration.

I found myself at a clothing store and went in to look around. I bought a few bikinis, a couple sun dresses, and an umbrella for the beach that came with a beach mat. I decided to go out to the beach and sit for a while, even if I wouldn't let my skin near the sun.

I found a shop that sold art supplies, along with other tourist needs, and bought a pad and pencil. I sat on the beach and did something I hadn't done in years. I still had the knack for it, even if the lines weren't so great now. The drawing came to life, and I was pleased with it, even if it was only a picture of the ocean and the golden sand in front of me.

It wasn't the drawing that was important; it was that I'd had time to do it that mattered. Normally, I was too stressed to sit and put pencil to paper. I'd wanted to draw my nieces and nephews since they were born, but my schedule had been too hectic for that. I'd never had time, and if I did have a moment, I took care of my errands and the most pressing needs. Drawing and relaxation hadn't been on that list.

Now, I'd have time to learn yoga and maybe even

start to paint again. I could practice on the piano, if I wanted to, and maybe even read a whole book. I hadn't stroked any keys in over a year, so I'd probably sound terrible, but who cared?

I had a new life, a new independence to get on with. So what if my brothers hadn't quite figured that out yet? They would; they weren't bad men after all. Just assholes, I thought with a forgiving smile. They couldn't help it if they'd been raised that way.

It was my father and mother's fault the boys treated me like that. Later, when I'd been old enough to say I'd wanted to do something else, they'd all ignored me. They'd just bulldozed over my tiny voice and kept going on with their plans. Not anymore. I'd change my phone number if that was what it took, but I would no longer be at their beck and call.

Not now that I was a woman. Well, almost, anyway. There was one final act to complete before I could say my womanhood was accomplished. I'd wait for Mr. Dark, and on that final night, if he still didn't want to break the contract, I'd push him until he did exactly what I'd want him to. I wasn't sure how yet, but I had some time to study up on the whole thing. I'd be prepared for battle the next time I saw him.

## 13

## DYLAN

*I* woke up slowly, confused about where I was. It didn't feel like my bed, but then, I was used to that. I traveled a lot, so being in an unfamiliar bed was common. Where was I?

My brain kicked in a little, and I remembered I was at Elmo's, not at home. I'd been with Stephanie and stayed the night with her. I could have gone home, but after what I'd put her through, I thought she'd need me to be there with her. I'd rocked her world, and I wasn't the least bit bashful about admitting it.

I swiped at my face to wipe the sleep away and then reached for her. My hand met empty air, and I turned my head to see the bed was empty. I thought perhaps she'd gone out for some reason, but then I saw a note on the table beside the bed. I rolled over, a smile on my face despite the fact that I'd woken up alone.

She'd been an intriguing little number, I'd give her that. I thought we'd have three consecutive days together, but she had gone home, <u>so I guessed it would be different days.</u> Or something like that … I needed coffee to think straight. I made a pot after I put my clothes on and washed up and thought about the night before.

She'd been eager, patient, but willing to say no. She'd been honest about what she'd wanted, and once she understood that she didn't have to be coy with me, she'd been very blunt about her desires. I'd wanted to push her, to find her limits, but I'd got lost in the way she responded to my touch and forgot the plan.

All I wanted from people was open honesty, without guile or wiles, and that was what Stephanie had given me from the start. She was innocent in some things; she was virginal in more ways than one, but she'd given me all I'd wanted from her. She was genuine from the start, and I admired that in her.

That wasn't to say I hadn't had my own mind blown. I'd become a little more than jaded over the years. I'd seen it all, done it all, but Stephanie had reminded me of what it was like. How wondrous each new exploration could be. I'd even felt nervous when I'd touched her, something she'd never know, but I did. She'd brought back the schoolboy days of uncertainty and indecision.

I left the room after I finished the coffee, spoke to an unknown woman at the front of the club, and left. I'd never been there that early in the morning and didn't know the woman, so I didn't hang around for a chat. By the time I made it to my car, I knew that three days wouldn't be enough, and I kind of resented Stephanie for that. I couldn't get her off my mind. The way she felt, her taste, the way she responded to me, all played over and over again in my head, until I was driven to distraction.

Once I made it home, I couldn't concentrate, no matter how many emails I tried to respond to. The place was new, I probably needed to settle in more than I had, but I'd tried to work to break the spell Stephanie had cast on me with her sweet sighs of surrender. I tried to watch the news on the television, but all I could see was the way her breasts lifted when she arched her back, and my dick was hard all over again.

I hadn't been this into a woman in my entire life. A few had intrigued me, but the fascination had ended quickly. I didn't have time, or the patience, for a long relationship, and I had no plans for a wife and children. I was a man of business who liked his occasional pleasure, that was it. Until Stephanie.

I sat back on the couch, my hand over my zipper, and squeezed as I thought about her. She'd been so ready for me, and that was part of the reason I'd denied penetrative sex to us both. I knew how badly she wanted to have me inside of her, because I wanted it just as much as she did. I knew she'd be slick and tight, and *fuck* ... I wanted a lot more time with her.

Was three days enough? Should I be worried that I wanted more than that with her? She was only a woman, I thought, why was she so different from the rest? Why was I on the verge of jerking off to her memory, when she'd only just given me a blow job a few hours before? I wasn't a teenager anymore, my dick and getting off were no longer my sole focus in life. Most of the time.

Today seemed to be different, and she'd turned me into the kid who couldn't stop playing with his dick, I thought with a soft laugh. I went into the shower and turned it on as I undressed. I was not going to jerk off on my couch, but the shower was fair game. I dipped under the spray and let the heat and moisture wash away the sore tension in my muscles. Making sure Stephanie got everything she'd asked for had left me with a few sore places in my neck and back, but fuck if it wasn't worth it.

I was really worried about how much I wanted to see her again, though. I wasn't that kind of guy and never had been. That was why I'd made it clear from the start, been as honest and open as I could be. An idea struck, and I washed off quickly.

By the time I was clothed again, I had a new plan. I'd fuck her out of my head with someone else. There was a girl at another club with black hair and the bluest eyes I'd ever seen. Her name was Michelle, and she had the perfect lips for sucking a dick. I texted her and found out she was free tonight, so I booked some time with her.

I sent Roxie a message to let her know I'd be busy tonight if Stephanie called, then decided to spend the rest of the day at the gym. I didn't really need the workout, but I couldn't maintain this body if I let myself go. I headed there and worked up a sweat to keep my mind off the woman with a sigh who could instantly make me hard.

I tried my best, and by the time I got to the place Michelle told me to meet her at, I was ready for a night of filthy sex. I'd fuck Michelle, and that would set me straight. She greeted me in a room above the club, and I could hear the music and felt it as a throb below my feet.

"Hi there, handsome. How are you tonight?" She was in a black halter dress that barely had enough shiny material to cover her bottom. The black stockings and six-inch stiletto heels created a dramatic effect that I couldn't look away from.

Her full, round breasts tantalized me through a slit that ran from her neck down to her belly button, and I wanted to feel the soft skin in my hands. "I'm alright, Michelle, how are you?"

"I'm good, Dylan. Want a drink?" She went to a cabinet, bent down, and opened a door to look inside. We have scotch, vodka, and gin. There's also a few sodas in there and some juice."

"Scotch please, Michelle." I took the drink she handed me, and she sat down beside me. "Where do you want to eat?"

"There's a new Mexican place just up the street..." She used a seductive voice that got my attention. Especially when she put her hand high on my thigh.

"Not quite what I had in mind, but it's your decision." I thought it was a bit heavy for a night that I had planned to spend in bed, but that was okay if that was what she wanted.

"It's my favorite food, so yeah, I'd like to try it." She took the now empty glass I handed to her and stood up. "Come on, we can walk to it."

The walk up was silent on my end, but she chatted away about her cats, and how she wanted to go a new dance club that had opened up. I wasn't one for dancing, so she'd have to wait for the next guy to do that. I wanted to eat, and fuck, that was all.

When we were seated, her attitude toward the waitress was a bit rude and imperial, as if I'd just taken her to a five-star restaurant, not a Mexican restaurant. That kind of irked me, but I let it go. Sex was all that mattered. My annoyance, however, rose, when Michelle began to order.

I had money to blow, but from appetizer to dessert, she ordered as if she'd gone through and chose each dish that cost the most. Something told me Stephanie wouldn't do that. She'd order what she liked, not what a price said was best.

"And please, don't forget to add extra cheese to the beans. I know how you people like to skimp on those things," Michelle said from her side of the booth. I looked at her and saw a snide sneer on her face.

Ugh, she was one of those people, I thought to myself and politely ordered my food without comment. She didn't want to let it go.

"I love Mexican restaurants, but they're always staffed by people who can barely speak English." Her pretty blue eyes rolled in a rather ugly way. "I don't know why they don't just hire Americans."

"From her accent, she sounded American to me." I pointed out. The fact that the woman had blonde hair and green eyes didn't mean she wasn't of Hispanic origin, but her accent was straight down home South Carolina.

"Oh, that doesn't mean anything." This time I was the recipient of her eye rolling extravaganza. "I bet they're all illegal too."

I stared at her, floored at her attitude. She didn't know the woman, or the hiring practices of the place, but she had already assumed so much. Maybe I should have just booked her for the time in bed and not have offered her dinner too. I'd met her a couple times at another bar Freddy took me to, and she'd seemed hot, intelligent, and fuckable. Now, I had to wonder.

The fact that every move she made, my brain compared to Stephanie didn't help. Thankfully, she stayed quiet as we waited for our food, and then the only conversation we had was about how good the food was. She had her extra cheese, and I imagined the waitress probably wanted to spit in it, so I left her a really good tip. Just for keeping her cool despite Michelle's demand for a new glass of wine because she'd managed to get a piece of cheese in it. Or the fact that she wanted different forks for her various dishes, a new tub of tortillas because her old ones had gone cold, and the moment when she sent her dessert back twice, because the apple pie wasn't hot enough.

I was ready to ditch her by then, but I told myself I wasn't here to like the woman and start a new relation-ship; I was there to fuck her and get Stephanie out of my system. Luckily, Michelle had a seductive body, and if she'd shut up, I might be able to rise to the occasion.

As soon as we were back in the room assigned to us, she pushed me against the door and kissed me aggressively. "I want you to fuck me right now, Dylan. Get those clothes off."

"Okay," I said and pushed her away. She needed a mint, which she'd refused after the dinner we'd had, and to tone down the dominance. That wasn't my game. Not with her.

"You need to hurry; I have another date in an hour," she said as I went to the couch to settle down.

I'd gone to sit there because I thought it would give her a minute to freshen up, but she followed me. "Did you pay already or are you paying after? I'm just wondering if you're going to leave a tip? I'm saving up for a trip to Hawaii."

"Oh. I have paid, but I can leave a tip too." She was really turning me off at this point, and I wanted to tell her to shut up and get my dick out of my pants for me.

"Goody!" she cried with glee, and I frowned. Seriously?

She sat beside me and pushed her face into my neck and grabbed at my crotch with her right hand. I jumped but let her work her technique on me. Nothing happened until she sighed, and my brain immediately remembered Stephanie's sounds. I was hard as a rock then, but not for Michelle.

"Oh, baby, you're ready for momma, aren't you? Does baby need a titty too?" She pushed the open panel of her dress aside and revealed a bare breast to me. Only, I didn't want to touch her at all now.

"Um…" I looked at her with an expression that I couldn't control. Her words disgusted me, and when she tried to press her breast in my face, I'd backed up. "No."

"What's wrong? Don't you want me?" She looked confused and a little miffed as she glared at me.

Michelle was obviously far too dominant for my tastes, and she had some odd kink that I wasn't into at all. I pushed her away and stood. "I'm sorry, I have to go. Not feeling well all of a sudden."

"But you haven't fucked me yet! You know we don't give refunds, right?" She bared her other breast, as if that would tempt me.

It might have if I hadn't spent an hour and a half at a restaurant with her, only to come back and have her start some mommy fetish with me. If she'd just stayed quiet, I might have been able to fuck her; I might have been able to stamp Stephanie out of my memory, but she just wouldn't shut up.

"It's alright, I don't need the money back. Take it. And here, this too." I took a $50 out of my pocket and handed it to her. "Thanks, but yeah, not feeling well."

Obviously, I wasn't going to get Stephanie out of my system that way. Maybe a week wasn't so bad. It wasn't long enough to form an attachment or anything. I needed to talk to Roxie. I'd fucked up; maybe I could fix the night before it was over with.

I thought about offering her two weeks but knew how easily I became bored. I couldn't get her out of my system with one night, but surely a week would do it? She was only a woman, after all. Right?

## 14

## EMILY

It wasn't any surprise that when I turned my phone on around five that evening it vibrated for a full five minutes. Mason had blown my phone up. I thought it would burst into flames before it finally came to a rest. I stared at it for a few seconds once it finally stopped, not sure it was done.

I opened the cover on it and pressed the button so the screen would come on. Mason had called, stalked my Facebook, Instagram; he'd even been on my Snapchat and sent me texts. He needed me; Laura was ill. I felt bad that I'd ignored my phone all day, when he'd truly needed me this time, but I hadn't been there.

"Mason, how's it going?" I asked once he'd picked up my call. I'd dialed him back as soon as I saw the message that Laura was in the hospital.

"Not so good, sis. We have the plane at the airport.

Can you make it back here tonight?" Mason sounded tired, even over the phone, and a pang of guilt pierced my heart.

"Of course, Mason." I thought about Mr. Dark, but I knew that could wait. "What have they said about her condition?"

"Her gallbladder has to come out. It's about to rupture, and if that happens, she'll have a much longer recovery and have a lot of procedures. I don't know; the doctor said so much I couldn't take it all in." I heard a note of panic in his voice and wanted to say, *this, this is when you call me,* but I didn't.

It wasn't the time for admonishments, it was the time to be a sister. "I'll pack a bag and head out in about fifteen minutes, Mason. Don't worry about the kids. I'll be there with them soon."

I could picture the little faces of Francesca, Nick, and Alex, confused and lost without their momma. They probably had no idea what was going on and were terrified for their mother. I'd be there soon enough to reassure them. Gallbladders weren't so bad, but if hers was bad enough it was about to rupture, she was in trouble. She was definitely in a lot of pain and probably had been for a long time. Which was probably why she had forgot my birthday, I thought as I drove to the airport. This wasn't something sudden; it was something she'd been dealing with for a while.

My mother had to have hers out when I was thirteen, and even as a teenager, I'd been afraid for her. I could remember how sick she'd been before it was removed, how much pain she'd been in. Poor Laura, and there I'd been like a whiny brat, having a fit because nobody remembered my birthday. Guilt wracked me, but I kept driving.

I'd make it up to her now and keep her children safe until she could take that job up again. It wasn't that hard; they were small children. They needed to be kept entertained, fed, and cared for, and I'd had a lot of prac-tice at that. I sat in the leather seat of the beautifully decorated jet and waited. The flight wouldn't take long, and I'd be in Charlotte before I knew it.

The trip was long enough that I had time to wonder about Mr. Dark and to think about the way I'd spent the previous night. Was he thinking of me? Remembering? I felt stupid for it, but I'd hoped he was. He'd offered me three days, but I wondered if I could talk him into more? Like him, I didn't want a relation-ship, or I'd have found a man some other way. I'd wanted an education, to be pleasured, and to get on with my life.

But was that all? He'd made me aware of what I'd missed out on my whole life, and now, I wanted to be greedy. I wanted it all, desperately. Maybe I should be afraid of myself, the need I felt, or afraid of him, and the things he planned to do. The things he made me want. I wasn't afraid, though, not with him.

He made me feel safe, secure, and empowered. Like I could say no if I wanted to. He made me feel as if I could make a demand that would be met. Like my input would have some relevance to a final decision. Like I'd found a missing piece of me with him. Or maybe he was that piece?

That was an even scarier thought, and I pushed it away. I didn't need to do something like fall in love with a man, just because he'd made me come. That was stupid. Anybody with the right skills could get a woman off. We were known to even get ourselves off. That wasn't love. That was appreciation. Or something like that; I wasn't sure what to call it exactly.

Freedom, perhaps? That sounded right, and I smiled a half smile. Imagine, finding freedom in submission. But I had, as I knew I would, from the moment I saw a woman in a video tied to a post. The expression on her face had been one of complete satisfaction, maybe even blissful. I'd known that was what I wanted right then. The whole scenario.

Tied down so I couldn't move, with someone else in control of what I did and felt. Even down to whether I moved or not. That had been so hot, when he'd tied me to the bed and told me not to move. I'd wanted to tell Mr. Dark I'd be his forever in that moment, but I knew it was stupid and had kept quiet. I'd kept still, as he told me to do.

A call came in on my Facebook messenger, and I answered it with a secret smile. "Hi, Roxie."

"How are you, baby?" Despite the fact that I was flying through the air, Roxie sounded as clear as a bell. I even heard the small laugh she gave as I groaned.

"I'm so sore now! But I don't mind. I earned that sore." I'd talked to her earlier, but I didn't mind going over it all again. I was doing that in my mind now anyway.

"He called me a little while ago. He canceled his appointment. Wants to know if you're available tonight?" She sounded pleased with herself again, as if she'd known all along he and I were meant for each other. At least for a short time.

"Damn!" I looked out the window as Charlotte came into view, a city of lights from above. "I had to come to Charlotte. My sister-in-law is sick and has to have surgery immediately. I promised I'd watch the kids."

"Oh, honey! You should definitely be there for your family. I totally understand! Can I do anything on my end? Do you need some plants watered or anything?" I could hear the concern and felt honored. Not many people earned Roxie's respect anymore, and for her to offer that meant a lot to me.

"No, I haven't had time to find any plants, so there's

nothing to worry over. An orange that might start to go moldy on the counter, but I can deal with that when I get back. Do you think he'll wait for me?" I knew she knew who I meant, although I didn't say his name.

Mainly because I didn't know it, and I didn't want to call him Mr. Dark where someone might hear me. It sounded silly when I wasn't in that environment or with Roxie alone. I did feel a thrill that he'd called for me so quickly. Obviously, he'd been pleased with my performance. That made my shoulders straighten, and my head tilted back with pride.

"I think he will. The fact that he called me right away means he's definitely interested and wants more of you, missy." She gave a throaty laugh, and I joined her.

"Damn, I didn't even do that much, if I'm honest. He did all the work," I said, and sighed. "But then, I guess that's the point, isn't it?"

"It is, indeed, sweetie. Listen, I have to go; Freddy's just come in. You call me later, alright?"

"I will. The plane's about to land anyway, so I should go. Take care. And thank you!"

"No problem, Em. Take care now." She hung up, and the plane started to descend.

I hated that part of flights, but I still couldn't stop as I watched the plane descend to the ground once more. I closed my eyes when I thought the tires should hit the ground and held my breath. When the tires held and didn't sling the plane sideways, collapse, or cause the plane to burst into flames, a crazy idea but still one I worried about, I took a deep breath and relaxed.

I was soon out of the airport, in a car my brother had sent for me, and at the house with two noisy children and a baby who wanted to sleep. I put Francesca down in her crib and took Nick and Alex into the family room to watch a movie. Mason had taken to fatherhood well, and one of his proudest moments was when he had this family room built. He'd thought of the children and had the room decorated with a zoo theme. Toy animals filled shelves, stood on their own as giant, almost life-sized giraffes and elephants, and were painted on the walls. Pastel colors made the room seem soft, and the over-stuffed wraparound couch in front of a giant television screen invited all to sit and relax.

The couch, in a muted brown shade, was wide enough to allow two adults to lie side by side, so it was big enough that both boys could surround me while we watched their favorite movie. Only they didn't really want to watch it.

"Aunt Emily? Will Mommy come home?" asked Nick, and I clasped him tighter to my chest.

"Of course, darling. She'll be in the hospital for a little while, but it won't be long at all really. You'll see." He was small enough that my kiss on his cheek didn't make him cringe. Rather, he burrowed deeper into my embrace. Alex, snuggled up behind me with a pillow under his head so he could see, squeezed tiny arms around my neck, as if he'd needed reassurance too.

Yes, this was what I'd wanted. To be needed, to be loved, but also, to be appreciated. The boys didn't know how to express that yet, they were too young, but those hugs, that need for reassurance, told me my presence was important to them. Now, if only I could teach my brothers that.

Mason had tried, but he'd called me when he'd needed me. That was all I'd ever wanted from them, though. I didn't want to be on standby, but if I was absolutely needed, if it was an emergency, I was more than willing to help.

The only problem was, I wanted to be at home, my new home. With Mr. Dark. I pushed thoughts of him away as a cartoon elk chased a wild duck through the forest in the children's movie the boys chose, and I tried to figure out what was happening in the movie.

It wasn't long before we were all asleep, warm and comfortable wrapped up together. I found myself in a dark room, with only a candle to light the darkness. I could see the chair and table were both white, but other than that, I couldn't see anything.

Then Mr. Dark appeared, and I tilted my head in his direction with a smile on my face. "Hello there."

I didn't react when my voice echoed. It seemed

appropriate for some reason, and I didn't pay attention to it. "Hello, Emily. How are you?"

A chair appeared on the side of the table he moved to, and the light expanded to encompass him as well. He looked delicious, and I wanted to curl into his lap, his arms, to forget the world existed. Nothing could get to me when I was with him, I was sure of it.

"I'm well, Mr. Dark." I took his hand when he offered it, and suddenly we were dancing on a cloud in the darkness. I had on a long, slinky black dress, and I pressed myself into him.

He was warm, and the resistance of his body felt so good. "You aren't afraid."

His voice broke into the peaceful place I'd drifted to, and I smiled up at him. "No, should I be?"

"Maybe. You don't know me, Emily. You haven't even told me your real name." I didn't point out that he'd just used it; I simply listened to him and then replied.

"You don't need to know my real name. Not yet. I just need what you give to me." I ran a finger down his smooth cheek that covered high cheekbones and perfect teeth. "I don't need to know anything more about you, other than the fact that I'm safe with you. I know that."

"Do you? Because you don't know me, Emily." He looked concerned, and I wanted to wipe that concern away.

"What do I need to know? I know how you make me

feel, and that you made me free. You let me be me. You taught me how to say no." Which was something I could barely do with my family. And then I could only do that recently. Well, I couldn't tonight, but this was an emergency, wasn't it?

"If that's all you require, then I won't trouble you about it anymore." He spun me around, and suddenly, I could hear music. I put my head on his shoulder and stepped through all the steps I'd learned in my many dance classes at school. He expertly guided me through the cloud, and I didn't even notice that we shouldn't be on a cloud.

I woke up when I finally started to wonder how we could dance on a cloud, and I took the boys up to their rooms to sleep. The dream lingered in my mind, and I smiled the entire time I was in the shower. I still smiled as I put on pajamas and went downstairs to watch another movie. If he'd wait for me, I'd have to ask Mr. Dark to give us more time together. We'd need it. Only another week or two, that was it. I didn't want to get attached to him, but I did want more time with him. Just a little more. I missed him.

15

DYLAN

She'd been gone for three days. I sat in a chair and glared at the dancer on the stage. It wasn't Roxie, and she was terrible. I knew she wouldn't last long. From the listless way she danced, it was obvious she had a drug problem. Miss Maples would pull the woman aside, have her treated, then offer her a job somewhere else. I'd heard a lot about how fantastic Miss Maples was from Roxie over the last few days as I waited for Stephanie to come home.

A family illness had cropped up, and she'd had to go home. That had put the damper on things, but I couldn't complain. She had family. I had two adoptive parents and no siblings. I didn't know what it was like to have to take care of nieces and nephews while your family member was sick.

It gave me time to come up with a new contract, and

to think about whether I actually wanted to give it to her. I was alright, really, the first few days. I did the contract, I worked, unpacked my apartment, and settled into it. Roxie said it would be a couple of days, at least. When she wasn't back on the third day, I started to wonder.

Had the sick family member been an excuse? Did she really just not want to come back? Had she got what she wanted and decided to leave? No, she was too curious to walk away.

"When's she coming back, Roxie?" I asked as the beautiful young woman came to sit beside me. "Why can't I have her phone number?"

"You know that's against the rules until you sign on as her protector. Until then, you contact her only through me." There was an edge to Roxie's voice that I wasn't about to argue with, especially when her eyebrow lifted, and she gave me the female version of the 'don't fuck with me' look.

"Fine." I sighed, and sank lower in my chair. Perhaps a little childish of me, but I was getting antsy. I wanted to feel her soft skin and smell her delicate scent. And fuck, her taste, I wanted to taste her so much.

"I could offer you another girl, if you'd like?" Roxie asked with a twitch around her nose that meant something, but I wasn't sure.

"No, I'll wait for Stephanie." I didn't elaborate on

why, and I wasn't about to. That was my business, not hers.

When a grin spread over her face, I knew I'd passed some kind of test, but it didn't matter. The only person who mattered was Stephanie; only, she wasn't here.

"Do you think it will be much longer?" My fingers tapped time on the tabletop, the blunt tips manicured with short nails that barely made a sound.

"I don't think so. The issue was sorted quickly and without too much of a problem. Stephanie should be back soon." Roxie smirked, she actually smirked, and I wanted to be upset, but I couldn't be. She was right to smirk at my antics.

I was acting like a lovesick idiot. Over a woman I barely knew. I inhaled deeply and went back to my conversation. "How's Freddy then?"

"Fine. He had to go to San Diego this week, but he won't be longer than that."

"So it's just us then?" I asked with a goofy leer meant to make her laugh.

"Very much so. And no, you aren't getting in my pants! Even if you are a handsome devil." She gave me a wink, and I laughed with her. "Buy me a drink, sailor?"

"Of course, my lady. What would you like?" The waitress was busy, so I went up to the bar to order two drinks, and we headed back to the table.

"Why are you here tonight if Freddy's out of town?" I sipped at my scotch and looked at her over the rim of the glass.

"It's my job to be here, no matter what I'm doing while I'm here. I have to help make sure things run smoothly. Keep the men in line, and the ladies some-times." Roxie's façade slipped for a second, and I caught a glimpse of a tired woman who needed a break.

I'd have to suggest to Freddy that he needed to take his lady on a vacation. She'd let her mask slip, for just a moment. Although, Roxie seemed to be one of a few who didn't hide her face away, she did have a mask on, I realized, all the time. It was a peaceful expression that hid just how tired she really was.

Then it was back in place, and she slugged back the shot of vodka before she took a slug of ginger ale to wash it down.

"Another?" I asked, and she shook her head eagerly.

"Please, I think I'll need it tonight. Big boy over there doesn't quite know how to take no for an answer. I've told him twice already to keep his hands to himself. If he does it again, he's leaving with broken fingers." Roxie's chin jerked in the direction of a man at a table alone.

He was a fairly hefty guy, with thinning hair and mean eyes. I didn't like the look of him. "I'm here if you need help."

I decided to stay the rest of the evening, or until the guy left, for Roxie. I didn't have to, I knew that, but she was becoming a friend, and I'd wanted to protect her. It was the decent thing to do, I thought.

The man walked to the bar when the waitress ignored his snapping fingers and glared over at Roxie as he did so.

"Why doesn't Miss Maples just kick him out, Roxie? He's a nuisance, and he's going to cause a problem. He's got that vibe about him, you know?" I didn't take my eyes off the man as he went to the bar, sat on a stool with a heavy sigh, and stared at the bartender as he made the man's drink.

"He's some bigwig and friends with one of our major clients. She doesn't want to offend the other client, so she's let him in. I don't think he'll last long. Maybe another half hour before he does something stupid. It'll cause problems for Miss Maples, but, what can you do?"

The man that I'd now dubbed Kid Dickhead in my mind smoothed back the fluffy, poorly colored blond hair that draped over his head to hide his bald spot as he hefted his way off the seat and made straight for Roxie.

Her eyes narrowed, and I saw her tense. It was subtle, but if you knew her, you could see the way her shoulders went back and up and how her jaw firmed up.

"I'll give you three grand, Roxie. That's my final

offer." His piggy lips were wet and made my stomach turn as he spoke.

"I told you no, Roger. Please, abide by the rules and leave me alone now."

"Who do you think you are? You're just a high-class hooker; who are you to tell me no? I'm Roger Updike. I can have whoever, *whenever* I want. In fact, go to a room now. I'll go talk to Miss Maples, and she'll set you straight." His eyes had lit up, and his fat tongue came out to wet already slick lips. "Go on, do what your master says, bitch."

"First of all," Roxie said as she rocketed out of her seat, "I told you to leave me alone. Second of all, that's not how any of this works. You don't demand anything, you fat fuck! Lastly, and most importantly, I already have a protector; I don't have to fuck you or anyone else. I wouldn't fuck you if you offered me a million dollars, much less your measly three grand. Now fuck off, Roger."

Her voice had been calm as she spoke to him; there hadn't been the slightest bit of quiver or fear in her tone at all. She was sure, confident, and calm, which worked to make her words even more cutting. Roger's swollen eyes narrowed as he glared at her, his lips pursed even tighter. "What the fuck did you just say to me, whore?"

I stood then, unbuttoned my suit jacket, and

intruded on the conversation. "The lady said to take a hike, buddy."

"I'm not your buddy, and she's not a lady. I'll bend her over this table and take what I want if she doesn't start to act right."

He was going to say more, but my fist connected with his jaw, and his head snapped to the side. He hit the floor with a soft thud, and I buttoned my suit jacket with a twist of my head to loosen my neck. "Get out. Now."

"You can't do that, I'm..." He choked on his words, and his eyes went round because I'd leaned down, pushed him back with my open palm, and glared at him.

"I said stay down. When Miss Maples arrives, she'll explain the rules to you again. Or you can choose to leave quietly, now. It's your choice."

He mumbled something but stayed where he'd dropped. I sat at the bar and waited for whatever fate decided to hand me. I didn't have the authority, not really, to tell the man to get out, but he'd been rude, uncivil, and extremely obnoxious to Roxie. I couldn't stand it anymore, and I'd decked him.

It didn't take long before Miss Maples was in the bar and had escorted the man out. From the little I caught, she'd banned him from the place, and he wouldn't be allowed back in. No, it didn't matter who he was or who he was friends with. He was no longer allowed into the place. He'd broken far too many of the rules, all at once, and he'd accosted a protected female. That was the worse violation of all, to her.

I took a deep breath as Roxie sat with me and made sure her hair was still in place. "I'm sorry you had to do that."

"I'd say I'm sorry I did it, but I'm not. That was uncalled for. All of it. And I'm sorry you had to deal with it."

"It comes with the job, sometimes, Dylan. Even Stephanie will have to deal with it at some point. We all get it from these guys who think the world owes them a blow job." She crossed her left leg over her right and leaned toward me. "The world is an ugly place for women, Dylan. Remember that."

Her eyes, always so beautiful and full of life, were dull now and filled with pain she'd never speak of. Not to me anyway. I wanted to pat her hand, or kiss her cheek, some way to give her human contact that wasn't sexual, but I didn't want to upset her more. I held myself back and gave her a commiserating smile.

"I can't pretend I understand the view of the world you've been given, but I know plenty of jackasses. I'm sorry you have to deal with that so much."

"Eh, as I said, it comes with the territory." I saw the

mask go back into place, and life came back into her eyes. "Not a big deal really, is it? Just a dick with something to prove."

"He shouldn't take that out on you. It's just rude." I straightened my suit jacket and reached for my drink. "It must be shit living in this world sometimes."

"You wouldn't believe how shit it can be. I was lucky." She paused, as if afraid to say the next words, but after a moment of appraisal, she decided I was worthy. "I ran away from home. You can guess why: drunk mom, drug addicted step-daddy; it wasn't nice. I slept on the streets for a while, until it got too cold, then I wound up at a strip bar, down in Charleston."

"I had no idea." She came off as a well-educated woman, with a good vocabulary and a quick intelligence that came with a sharp wit.

"I worked hard to go to school when I could. I did some business classes and used the money I earned stripping to pay for it. Then I found out there was a difference between a stripper and a pole dancer. I fell in love with that, as an art form, as an exercise, and well, I eventually ended up here."

She didn't look as if she felt sorry for herself, but she did look pleased. She'd had a lot to overcome, and she'd done it.

"Yeah, but why aren't you an owner in this place, rather than a dancer? I mean, I know you still do competitions, and such, but why aren't you resting on the money from that?" I had been curious for a while, and I hoped she'd give me an answer now.

"I am, actually. I own one-quarter of the business, Miss Maples owns half, and we have an investor who prefers to remain hidden. I don't do this because I have to, Dylan. I like the lifestyle I have, the arrangement I have with Freddy, and the way I live now. I'm not some put-upon angel in need of a savior. And neither is Stephanie, by the way. She's here for the same reason as I am; she wants to be."

"Are you sure about that?" I asked, a rare moment of doubt.

I wasn't the kind for second-guessing myself, but that was before I met Stephanie. She had me questioning quite a bit about my life. I wasn't sure that was a good thing, but that was how it was at the moment, so I didn't resist too much.

Miss Maples made her way into the bar, a mysterious woman in a dark red gown who would have suited one of the queens of the silver screen early days of film, but it fit her perfectly. Every curve was delectable, and the lines were long and sensual, sure to hold the gaze of any viewer. She sat at the table, uninvited, and she didn't care a whit that she had interrupted.

"Thank you, Dylan, for your restraint. Violence is

prohibited, but in this case, it was also well-deserved. I appreciate your assistance."

I started to reply, but she stood, an impish smile in place, and left me to stare after her. A movement by the door caught my eye, and my body responded instantly with a surge of desire. Stephanie was back.

## 16

# EMILY

*I* walked up to him, my hips swinging seductively, and knelt in front of his chair, mask in place. "I'm home, sir."

I made sure my lips smiled prettily, and that my eyes were down, a sweet pose of submission I'd spent the day practicing; only he wouldn't know that.

Mason had found a nanny for the kids now that Laura was out of the woods, and I'd come home early this afternoon. I'd spent the hours preparing myself for him, for the man I'd dreamed about every night since I'd left him. I'd wanted this to be perfect. I'd talked to Roxie and when I'd arrived at the club I'd gone in to change my clothes and do my hair.

My hair was easy, it fell in straight, golden sheets down my back. The dress was the hard part. She'd put a pure white satin gown out for me, and a red one, with a strapless top that would fit my form exactly because the fabric was stretchy. I chose the white one because of the shimmer and the purity the white symbolized.

I decided then that I'd only wear white when I was with him. Until I was no longer a virgin that is. I wanted to change the contract. I wanted sex to be a part of that contract, and to remove the article about no penetrative sex. I wanted it to be him; it had to be him.

Now, I sat in the soft material, sweet and innocent, yet naughty. I glanced over and saw Roxie give me a wink of appreciation as she left the table. My dark lover didn't even notice she'd gone, he was so captivated with the picture I presented him with.

"Hello, pet," he said softly, and a shiver crawled down my spine at his words and the seductive tone of his voice. I'd *really* liked that.

He sat up, one knee on each side of me, and his hand came down to feel my hair. He let the strands play through his fingers, and I looked into gray eyes with a challenge in mine.

"Hello, Mr. Dark. I've missed you."

Mr. Dark gave me a knowing smile as his fingers trailed down my jaw. I turned my head into his hand, and he lifted my jaw to bring my gaze to his. The moment was gentle, calm, but I felt my heart skip a beat when I found his eyes full of pleased happiness.

"I've been waiting on you." An admission I hadn't

expected, but it filled me with delight. If I had a tail it would be wagging now.

"Shall we go to our room?" It was a suggestion, but it was also an admission that I was eager to be alone with him.

He held out his hand and pulled me from the floor to follow him to the room. I waved a goodnight to Roxie then turned back to him, the center of my attention for the rest of the night. He pulled me into his arms and pushed me against the door, and I opened my mouth to take the kiss he gave me. Eagerly, our tongues twined together, and I felt desire, familiar now, but still new and addictive, rise within me.

I wanted to tear his clothes off, to have him take me right now, here in a wild moment of senselessness. But, he pulled away, a grin on his lips.

He dropped his suit jacket on the floor then tore the shirt away from his hard stomach and off of his arms, the buttons gone in every direction. My nostrils flared, and my eyes narrowed as I looked at him. My fingers ached to touch him, but he stood too far away. He caught his lip between his teeth and gave me this look.

God, I desperately wanted him to fuck me! Again, though, he danced away, and I could only sink against the door with a groan. "What are you doing to me?"

"I'm enticing you, pet, showing you what you've missed. Don't you want to see?" His hand traveled down his stomach to the buckle of his belt, and my eyebrows knitted together.

"Yes, yes I do want to see." I was the one biting a lip now as I waited for the leather belt to fly from its loops and across the room.

"Let me touch you." I asked softly, bewitched, and he came over, the top button of his trousers undone but not the zipper. Too much of a temptation to resist.

I slid my hand up his rigid length as he came near, a hand on each side of my head as I cupped him in my hand and sank to my knees. Eager to please, but more eager to taste, to feel desire rocket through me as he groaned above me, his cock grinding into my mouth. I kissed the flat plane of his stomach, and our eyes met when I looked up at him.

I was his sole focus, the center of his world now, and I gave him a wicked grin.

"What's amused you so much, pet?" he asked, his finger on my cheek.

"I'm just happy to be with you, sir. Happy to know you want your cock in my mouth."

I felt a sense of power when I saw him shiver, his eyes on my face as I undid the zipper of his pants. He didn't reply now; he just watched me. His pants fell from his body, and I smiled to find him naked and ready for me. I lifted a hand, wrapped my fingers around him, and took a deep breath.

He felt nice in my hand, heavy and hot, silky smooth and thick. My index finger wouldn't meet my thumb, he was so thick, and I knew I was a lucky girl. My first time wouldn't be with a small man, at least. If he let me have my way, that is. I began to move my hand, not to provoke a reaction, but just to feel him, to feel the miracle that was the human body.

"Pet … what are you doing?" His voice was shaky, and that made me twinge deep inside, a secret happiness at the control I had over him for a moment.

"I'm pleasing you, sir." I let my tongue dance along the length before I spoke again. "Don't you want me to please you?"

I blinked up at him, innocently, coyly, and he shuddered with excitement.

"Don't stop." He wanted more. Good. I didn't want to stop.

"If that's what you wish, sir." The words came out as a sigh against his length. I leaned forward then, dragged my tongue over the tip of him, and learned his shape all over again, before I took another deep breath.

I opened my mouth, made sure my lips were slick, and took him inside my mouth.

Mr. Dark sighed, and his fingers plunged into my hair when I took him deeper. I wasn't an expert, but I'd watched some how-to videos once the kids were asleep and practiced the technique on him. He went deeper, further, and his finger trailed a gentle caress along my jaw. Something about that was sensual, knowing that his cock was in my mouth as he touched my face.

"Have you been practicing, Stephanie?" It wasn't an accusation, just a simple question.

"Does it matter?" I wiped at my face and smiled, ready to continue, compliant, and quiet.

"No, but if you want to know what I like, how to make it really good, I can guide you." He waited for my reply, and I could tell he wasn't judging, just asking if I wanted guidance.

"That might be helpful."

"Okay."

"What is lesson one?" I gripped him and gave a soft tug that was still firm enough to make his head sink back.

"Just like that, Stephanie." I tightened my grip on him a little more and listened to the way his breathing changed. "Do you want my mouth on your cock now?"

"Not yet. Fuck, don't stop." His words were a hiss, and I felt that twinge all over again.

"You just tell me when you want to stick your cock in my mouth, sir, and I'll let you in." That was really just a tease and nothing more. I was getting the idea about how to tease a man into passion.

His eyes cut down to my lips, and his fingers teased at them. "Open, Stephanie."

That was definitely a command, and he held my chin as I opened my lips for his entry. My tongue snaked out to lick at the thumb still on my chin as I moved my head forward.

I opened my lips to him, and he moved forward to thrust into my open mouth with precision. He didn't miss at all, and I closed my mouth around him but didn't move. I wanted his instructions.

"Now, suck me, Stephanie. Suck my dick." At any other time, I'd have slapped him then shuddered at his crudity, but right now, it only enhanced the delight I felt, my desire.

I pulled my cheeks in and sucked at him as I worked my way up his length and let my tongue cup him from the bottom.

I placed my hand at the base of his cock, circled around his girth to hold him in place as I went back down. I increased my pace every time his breath hissed in between his teeth or he groaned, until I heard him moan and fall back against the door. Then, I kept doing what I was doing, lost in the sounds he made in the way he thrust into my mouth.

Mr. Dark's hips moved in time with my head, his thrusts not gentle at all. He'd lost control, and he moved in time with my mouth's suction.

"Fuck. Stephanie." My lips were going numb, but I

didn't care, so when he pulled away, out of my mouth way too quickly, I protested.

"Why did you stop?"

"Later, Stephanie. I want to look at you." I was confused until he moved, and I stepped back. I fell onto the bed, and he followed me until he reached the edge. His fingers traced up my legs and to my thighs. "Open."

I thought he was going to fuck me, to finally do the one thing I wanted most from him, but he didn't; he just traced the insides of my thighs and pulled my hand down to him as his fingers traced my folds.

He'd positioned himself at the side of the bed, and I soon figured out he wasn't going to fuck me. Instead, his lips met the sensitive skin between my legs, and his tongue slid along me until he found just the right spot.

"Fuck! Oh fuck, that's it. No, fuck no, don't stop!" He'd found my clit and paused, until I repeated fuck far more than I ever had before. Then, when I'd urged him on enough, his tongue flicked at me, and I lost every thought in my head. He moaned and thrust into my hand, so I gripped at him, not really paying attention.

My nipples tightened, and I tugged at them with my empty hand which didn't ease the ache at all; it only made it worse, and I cried out in frustration, my hips a wild wave of movements as his tongue fucked with my head.

I was on the verge of an orgasm, I knew that now;

he'd taught me well in our short time together, and I held my breath as the pressure built inside of me. Tight, good, it felt like it would consume me, if I didn't soon explode. I panted, I mewled, I did it all until, at last, I felt that rush, the flutter that soon spread to my entire body, straight up to my brain.

I heard a grunt of satisfaction, but I didn't care as again and again waves pulsed through me, throughout my entire body. My back was bowed, my nipples were as tight as they'd ever been, and my pussy absolutely convulsed within me. I felt as if I was about to turn inside out, or I'd die, but it was too good to stop. I was not me; I was only what he allowed me to be, until I didn't even think I existed anymore. I just was.

"Once you've recovered, my dear, we can take care of me."

"You smug fuck!" I tried to say, but it only came out as a croak of laughter. I rolled the arm over my eyes up enough to glare at him as I came back down to earth. His succulent lips trailed across my hot thighs, and he inhaled my scent, before he swiped at me again with that tongue of his and made me jump. "Stop, you bastard!"

He laughed as he got up and came to rest beside me in the bed. "Aren't you hurting?"

"I am, but I'll live. I want you to be relaxed. I've missed you." His nose pushed into the soft skin of my neck, and he kissed me. "I'm glad your family is better, but I missed you."

Ah. I'd wondered what Roxie had told him. Mostly the truth apparently. Good, there'd been no reason to lie. He rolled over into me, into my heat, and I felt him still hot and hard against my hip.

"I think we need to take care of this problem for you. It looks painful." I slid down his body, determined to finish the job this time.

"If you like. As much as I want that pussy of yours, as much as I want to be buried up to my eyeballs in it, I can't be. We have a contract that says that's a rule we can't break. So fill your boots."

I closed my eyes as I took him into my mouth, the rigid length a scrape against my teeth. I opened my mouth wider, to minimize that, and he sighed in happiness. I opened my mouth more and took him deeper as he invaded my mouth. A shudder passed through him when he hit the back of my throat, and I could take no more. I tried to breathe through my nose, but he blocked me, and I moved, so that I could breathe. I wanted to take all of him, but damn if he wasn't huge.

"Look at me, Stephanie." I opened my eyes to see his glittered with an icy gray fire. What was that look in his eyes? Was it the look any man had when a woman sucked his cock, or was there something more there?

Would he be receptive to a longer contract? He wanted to fuck me, but he was still banging on about the contract. Then his hands were in my hair, over my mask, and I needed to concentrate as Mr. Dark took control and began to fuck my mouth with groans of pleasure.

I pursed my lips and made sure my teeth were out of the way as he lost his ability to go slow and picked up the pace.

I found that if I squeezed just right, the pressure of my thighs would create a friction against my clit, and it felt good. With every single one of his gasps or groans, that pleasure increased, and I knew I'd soon be coming along with him.

Our breaths came together, timed just right to synchronize, and the quick gasps followed the pattern of his hips into my face. We weren't joined together, this wasn't what I'd had planned, but it was what was on offer, so I took. Together we reached for the release that we both craved. I just didn't expect to find it by squeezing my thighs together while I sucked his cock.

My brain went dark, but I still managed to not bite him as a moan broke out of my throat. Mr. Dark must have taken that as a signal because I heard a low grunt just as I felt a surge travel the length of him, and he gave a low shout of release. "That's it Stephanie, take it baby, take my come."

I eagerly swallowed and sucked, even as I felt the last wave of pleasure pass through me.

He let it play out, and I didn't pull away. Not until he pushed at my head, ready for me to stop sucking him now. I moved up beside him and sprawled out. "Fuck, how can that be so good?"

My skin was flushed hot, and I could feel sweat on my face and in my hair. I was too hot now, and I was glad I was at least naked now. I wasn't sure when or how that happened, but it had. The gown was on the floor, my shoes kicked away somewhere. "How did I get naked?"

"You tore the dress off and threw it away right before you sucked my dick the first time. Then your underwear went. I'm not sure when you took those off." He laughed and looked at me, his face tired.

"It doesn't matter." I sighed and just laid there, spent for the moment. And happy to be back with him. I wanted it to last forever.

17

---

DYLAN

 woke up before Stephanie and looked in the fridge for some orange juice but didn't see any. I dressed and went out to the bar to get some. I came back in quictly, saw she was still asleep in bed, and poured two glasses of the cold drink before going back to the bed.

I undressed, pulled back the covers, and slid into the sheets with her. This bed was much better than the one at my apartment, I thought as my muscles began to relax. I'd have to find out what it was and buy one for myself.

I turned in the bed and brushed Stephanie's hair back from her face. I wanted to ask her for a longer contract; I'd given up on trying to talk myself out of it. This woman was more than just a fuck I could forget about. She had class, and she made me think. She also made me hard as fuck, and I wanted her. I just wanted to know how far I could push her before she'd break first. I needed to find out tonight, so I brushed at her cheek until she woke up.

"Hi," I said softly once she woke up and smiled at me. Her fingers moved to re-tie the mask, but it had barely moved at all.

"Hi yourself," she said while she moved her hands up to the mask. "I'm wasting the night away, aren't I?"

I'd watched her with interest as she tied the ribbons all over again. I wanted to know what was hidden behind that mask. To see all of her face.

"You needed to rest. I'd like to take things a little further tonight, if you don't mind? Do you remember the safe words?"

Her face went still behind the mask, but there was curiosity in her eyes. "Yellow and red. Not so hard to remember."

"Good. Drink this. I think you'll need it."

She shifted in the sheets, and I felt her smooth leg slide up beside mine before she sat up. She tucked the sheet around her chest and reached for the glass I held in my hand. She took a sip and licked her lips. "What do you have planned then?"

I ran a hand up her silky skin, stopped at her shoulder, and studied her perfect skin. Creamy, pale, but with a peach tinge, she was beautiful. "I want to break you, pet."

"Pardon?" she asked, her juice forgotten.

"Drink up." I guided the glass back to her mouth. "It's only a test, one that we can stop at any time."

"Alright." She had no idea what she'd agreed to, but she was brave, interested; I'd give her points for that.

Once she'd finished her juice, I pulled her from the bed and guided her to the memory foam rug, pressed her down, and asked her if she was ready. "Do you need to go the bathroom, have an itch on the bottom of your foot maybe? Once you're in the restraints, I won't let you out until you say the safe word, or we finish for the night."

She took a deep breath, thought about it, and smiled a wobbly smile. "I'm ready to begin."

"Good. Give me your hands."

"Yes, sir," she said without prompting and gave me her hands, palms up. I lifted them over her head, pulled a pair of handcuffs from the bureau beside us, and then another as I attached each hand to a ring on the wall. I pulled her hands to test how far she could move and stepped back.

"How do you feel?" I watched her face for signs of fear or anxiety, but she seemed alright.

"I feel like I've always waited for you, sir." I wasn't

expecting that much honesty, but it gave me hope that this wouldn't end with her disappearing in tears.

Sometimes, people went into this lifestyle with blinders on, and I needed to know if Steph was a true sub or not. I thought she was, but I had to know. "I'm going to start with a feather, okay? And we'll work our way up."

"Of course," she said and raised her head. Her feet were flat against the floor, and her hands were over her head. I knew that her arms would begin to ache shortly, that the pain would distract her, and it was my job to keep her attention for now, if I wanted to give her the real experience she'd said she wanted.

I ripped the plastic from the gaudy purple ostrich plume and pulled it from the bag. "This is just to gauge how sensitive your skin is," I told her as I ran the feather over her skin. Goose bumps came up immediately, and she took a deep breath. Very sensitive to touch then.

"Very good so far." I wanted to kiss her but held back; I needed to explore her further. I moved the feather to her naked breast, firm and proud, and her eyes closed immediately. "Alright. I want to try something else."

Her nipples were very sensitive indeed, and I found a box with little suction cups. "I'm only going to leave these on for a few minutes. If it hurts, if you want me to stop, you know that you can say it. You also know that means we're done for the night and play will stop."

That was an incentive, to make sure she really wanted me to stop. She'd push herself to keep going past her limits if she knew it would all end and not make me stop at a moment of frustration for her.

She looked up at me, her hair around her shoulders and down her back. I loved the roundness of her hips, the tiny expanse of her waist, and how she looked cuffed to the wall. I was hard for her, too hard, but I knew this was a game that required patience, and I'd play it out.

I pinched a nipple suddenly, without any warning, and once it was hard, I placed the suction cup over it. I did the same with the other and then went down to my knees, "Open."

She spread her knees, but she looked confused. "What are you doing?"

"Adding one to your clit. In about two minutes you're going to start begging." I pumped the nipple suckers a little more, to make sure they stayed on despite the pump hanging from her side, and then focused on the pump on her clit. This one had a vibrator attached, and I knew this would be tonight's torment. "Now, I don't want you to come; do you understand, Stephanie?" Her cheeks were flushed already, and her head had that arrogant tilt I'd noticed before. I'd get rid of that arrogance soon enough, but only temporarily.

When I turned on the vibrator, she began to tense up, but then she relaxed. Another notch higher and her breath changed. One more and she hissed, and her eyes closed. Perfect. "Don't come, Steph. Be a good girl for me, or I will spank you." I ran a hand down her back and gave her ass a light slap, openhanded, so I knew it would bring the blood to the skin. It would tingle and drive her mad because she couldn't soothe it, but it would also be a nice burn, if she liked pain.

"I'm so hard for you, Stephanie. And you look so beautiful chained to this wall. I want to fuck you so bad. But you said no, and no it is." I put a finger over her lips. "Don't speak, unless it's a safe word; understand?"

She looked uncertain for a moment, but then she nodded in agreement. "Good girl."

My hand moved to the other globe of her ass and slapped. Her hands pulled at the cuffs this time, her back arched, and she moaned loudly. Oh yes, she liked a little pain with her pleasure. "Feel good, pet? Do you want more?"

She nodded, and I slapped her red skin once more, only lightly, but just enough. I was even harder now, but it could wait. "And now, pet? Do you want more?"

She nodded eagerly, and I wondered about putting a ball gag in her mouth, but I thought that might be too much. For now.

I pumped up the suction on her nipples, and she gave a very loud moan. "Don't come, pet."

A reminder that was also a punishment, because I also notched up the vibrating sucker on her clit. She opened eyes full of need, pain, and ecstasy. She was loving this as much as I was. I came up close to her and ran my hand along her bottom. I couldn't see it, but I knew one would have my handprint on it. I slid my hand between the globes, down to the puckered entrance there. "And what about here, pet? Is that part feeling empty too?"

Her eyes opened wide, shocked at my touch, but she only watched me. I knew her heart must be racing and checked. Yes, I could see the pulse in her throat beating rapidly. I pushed my finger in, just a little, and her eyes closed, and I heard a closed-mouth scream. "Mr. Dark."

"Ah ah!" I admonished as I cranked up her nipple suckers until her hips twitched. "No speaking, pet."

She groaned in frustration and pulled at the restraints, but she didn't give up. "Now, those suction cups can only stay on your nipples a little while longer, Stephanie."

I ran my lips up her neck slowly, to speak into the back of her ear. "I'm going to explore that ass of yours a little more first."

I found a pack of lube, slicked up a finger or two, and

slid my hand down the crevice of her bottom, until I found my goal. "Open your eyes, Stephanie."

She opened her eyes, and there was pain now, pain from her shoulders, from her frustration, and trying not to speak and move, and I could see it was fucking with her brain. I was going to make it worse, I thought with a little glee. I wanted her to come, but only when I said she could. Only when I let her. I wanted to know she could obey.

"You didn't say anything about your ass, my dear. I have to assume I can't fuck it with my dick, but my finger can, right?" I slid it into her heat, only up to the second knuckle, just enough to make her gasp loudly before she clamped down, trying not to come. Trying very hard not to come all over me and herself. "Oh, look at you. Trying so desperately not to let go. You want to come don't you, pet? You want me to shove that finger don't you?"

I could see it in her gray eyes, she wanted it very much, but she couldn't say it; she couldn't speak, because she was my toy for the moment, and she knew it. Her breathing increased, and I saw the way her hips started to twitch when I began to jab that finger in and out of her ass, and I knew she was right there. Just on the precipice.

"You want to come desperately, don't you, pet?" I

growled low against her ear. "Oh, you want it so bad. Almost as much as you want my dick."

Another twitch and a whimper. She looked at me, her eyes full of frustrated tears, her lips pressed together to say words, safe words, and I thought, perhaps, I'd pushed her too far. I waited, but she took a deep breath and closed her eyes. This was it, either she'd break to my will or break to her fears. It was seconds away and her choice to make.

Her head dropped, at last, and I knew I'd won. She wanted to beg, but she'd just pushed into a new zone, a level many people couldn't make it to. One of control that was about to snap, but still she held on. Because I'd told her to. I released the suction on her cups all at the same time then pulled my finger from her ass as I stood up. She looked up at me, tears in her eyes, but she didn't ask the words on her lips.

I let her hands down from the cuffs and took her to the bed. She squirmed as blood rushed around to parts that had been constricted only moments ago, and I told her to wait while I cleaned my hands. She didn't complain; she just waited until I came back and made sure her mask was still in place. "Bend over, pet."

She didn't even hesitate. She bent over the bed, her ass at just the right height, and I ground myself into her heat for a moment. It felt so good, that pressure and her damp heat on my cock, but I pulled away. "No vaginal sex."

I turned so I was sideways to her and quickly smacked her ass on both sides, a little roughly, and my reward was a moan. I brushed my fingers down from her ribs then back to her ass. Another pop of my hand, another moan, but this time, her hips twitched. "Do you know why I denied you an orgasm just then, pet?"

She shook her head no, and I smiled. A very quick learner.

"To teach you to control yourself. You come only when I tell you to come."

"Yes, sir," she said, and I lifted an eyebrow. She'd done that deliberately, but it was her job to provoke me, to test me. A very sharp slap on the ass this time, and she hissed.

"No speaking," I admonished, and she nodded. "Good girl."

I bent then and opened her folds. With a rough grip on her thighs, I pulled that juicy pussy to my face, and sucked at her clit hard and fast. It was still sensitive, still on edge, and it took seconds to have her grinding on my face. "Come now, Stephanie."

And so she did.

18

— ⁘ —

## EMILY

"**W**ould a bath be in order?" he asked from behind me. I still shook from the things he'd done, from the things he'd made me feel.

It hadn't taken long, but then I was primed. I hadn't seen him in days, and my body wanted his touch more than anything else in the world. I hadn't known suction cups could provoke so much pleasure. When he'd placed the first one on my nipple, I'd fought not to squirm. The second one had nearly done me in. When the third one was applied, a battle began.

Then, the rest. I'd been pushed beyond arousal and straight into a new world of pleasure so quickly, with a speed I didn't understand, and when he'd invaded me back *there*. A shiver shook me all over again, and I turned around. "Yes, I think a bath is just what I need, sir."

He nodded and went to the bathroom. I heard the taps come on, and the bathtub began to fill. I thought about what I'd said, the way sir came off of my tongue so easily. Readily, even. Was it because I didn't know his name? Was that what made it so easy?

"You'll have to take off your mask," he reminded me when he came back in.

I reached up for the cloth, unsure for a moment, but then I removed it. He looked at me, took in a deep breath, and smiled.

"You're beautiful, but I knew you would be." His fingers traced around my eyes and down my cheek.

"Thank you." I knew I'd rarely been photographed, and that he wouldn't be likely to know who I was, so I decided it would be fine for him to know my face. I'd put it back on before I left the room, however.

"Come, let me help you in." He didn't need to guide me to the tub, but he did.

I sank into the water with a deep sigh. Sore muscles relaxed, and the steam made me sleepy. I slid down until only my head was out of the water in the deep, antique porcelain tub. He sat on a stool beside me, and I held my hand out to his.

For a moment, my bottom remembered where those hands had been and what he'd done. Was it penetrative sex, what he'd done? I was sure it was, but I wouldn't argue it. It had felt too good to protest, and it wasn't like he'd got off inside me.

That made me wonder … we hadn't had time to talk about contracts, but maybe later. Right now, I wanted to know he was pleased with me.

"Can I do anything for you, sir?" I asked, and I stared up at him wide eyed. I wanted to look as innocent as possible, because he seemed to react to it instinctively. My inexperience excited him, and that excited me.

"Later. For now, just relax, Stephanie."

I heard music beginning to play and saw he'd turned a small mp3 player on that rested on a shelf in the large bathroom.

Before long, he began to move around, and he ducked my head under the water to wet my hair. He massaged a beautifully scented shampoo into my hair, before he gently rinsed it away. After that, he scrubbed me down with a washcloth and made sure every part of me was clean. When I got out, he wrapped me in a warm, fluffy white towel that reached down to my calves.

"I haven't forgotten, Stephanie," he said as he pulled me out of the bathroom.

"Forgotten what, sir?" I wasn't sure what he'd meant.

"I haven't finished. But I will." He led me to the bed, and I crawled up on it to spread out naked to his eyes only.

"I will not fuck you, my lovely, but I will make us both come." His slim fingers trailed down my flat stomach, down my bare pubis, and slid into my folds. My heart sped up as I watched his fingers move along my skin. When his finger teased my slick entrance, my eyes opened wide and lost focus.

I gave a ragged moan, and Mr. Dark moved his tongue, a wet slide, over my pale pink nipple. I felt his tongue rasp at the tip again, and I began to purr. Mr. Dark scraped his teeth against me gently, his lips on my nipple, a delight I could not resist.

He moaned, and he pressed his cock into my slim hips to coax me to explore him, to explore his needs. My hand fluttered down to his cock, and he gasped as I found him, and his eyes closed as his cock grew even harder in my hand.

I sighed my own pleasure and smiled when Mr. Dark glanced up at me. His fingers moved down between my thighs, where he started to tease at me, to circle around the entrance that he knew I wanted him to explore.

My hips began to circle in the same pattern, and he matched his pace to the pace of my hips. I wanted to fall back and enjoy the moment, but I knew he hadn't received his own pleasure yet. It wasn't fair that I'd come so much, and so hard, but he hadn't had anything yet.

We had set rules, though, and he'd made that one

rule his own. He would not penetrate me, at least vaginally, and he had no intention of breaking that rule. He
soon distracted me from my thoughts when he leaned
over to kiss me, and my eyes closed. There was only the
faint light from the bathroom to guide our hands, but it
was enough.

"I need to be inside of you, Stephanie. I want it so
much. But you made it a rule." He gasped out the words
and brought my attention to him again. "I need to feel
your heat around me, the way your slick walls will grasp
at me, but not tonight. Fuck, not tonight."

"Do you want my mouth?" I asked and made to
move.

"No, I need to make you come, to make you want my
dick inside of you, to make you beg for it."

With a low growl, he moved and pushed me back as
he fell to the floor to his knees. I gasped when his teeth
grazed my clit softly, and my hips jerked up to meet his
touch.

"Mr. Dark, I already want you to fuck me," I gasped
out above him, but it didn't come out right. The sound
of my voice turned into a low moan, and my back
arched. My hips moved of their own will, and my
fingers buried in his hair.

His tongue danced on me there, hot and wet, an
indescribable feeling that I didn't want to end. I knew it
would lead to more pleasure, but right now, that sensa-

tion of his tongue on me was enough; it was too good to turn away. Then he took it a step further.

Mr. Dark sucked my clit hard and fast, and it reminded me of the suction cups, the way the vibration added to the sensation, and I didn't care if I looked stupid or not. I bucked against his face and pressed my shoulders into the bed to feel more, to have more.

"Fuck, that feels so good." I didn't know my words would require a response. They were just words, something I'd said without really meaning to.

"Just imagine what it would feel like with my thick cock inside of you, Stephanie. How full you'd be, every nerve touched, fucked, as your clit is sucked. I could put all of those delightful little cups on your body while I fuck your tight little pussy."

His finger had replaced his mouth, but it wasn't as good. I needed that suction of his mouth. I wanted to demand he give it back, but I knew I'd be punished if I did. I heard the dare in his voice.

"I'm going to fuck you so hard soon enough, Stephanie. I'm going to get my cock in you, and I'm going to ride you until you can't take anymore." Then he went back to my clit, and his tongue flicked at the button, stabbed at it, until I couldn't hold on anymore and totally abandoned all dignity.

"Do it, Mr. Dark, fuck me, please; oh god, just fuck me." I had no idea what it would feel like, but the way he described it, the way I ached in there, for something more, I knew it would be all I wanted it to be.

He dug into the globes of my ass with his fingers, to add an edge of pain to my pleasure. I gasped, that sting just enough, almost. A little more … and I was off.

I began to contract around him, my thighs clamped against his head, and I groaned loudly as my body twisted in relief. He went with it, his fingers still tight on my ass as I begged for more in my mind.

"Please…" I begged for more, for all of it, the whole Mr. Dark experience, but he wouldn't budge. His tongue stayed in place, until I finally slumped against the bed. Fulfilled but still empty.

"I'll give you this much, Stephanie." He pulled me to his hips, his cock trapped between us, and I felt him slide through the slippery silk of my body.

Instinct made me tilt my hips, made me twist to try to take him inside of me, but he growled and grasped at my hips. "Stay still or I'll stop, turn you over, and spank you, Stephanie."

I went still and waited. I could tell from the tightness of his jaw and the way his teeth barely opened that he was about to lose control. His cock nudged at my opening, and he groaned with frustration. So close, just a tilt, and he'd be inside of me. But he moved and started a slick pace, slow at first, but faster as he found a rhythm he liked.

"Tell me how much you want it, pet." He moved his hips, the head of his cock barely there, just a pressure that was almost inside of me, and my fingers grasped at the bed covers. A quick thrust and he'd be inside of me, but his eyes pinned me in place. I didn't dare move, not with that look in his eye. "Tell me pet. Tell me how you want me to fuck you."

"I want you hard and fast, Mr. Dark. I want you to fuck me like men fuck women in those videos. Deep and slow, hard and fast, I want it all, so long as you fuck my pussy until I can't walk the next day. Can't you, just this once? Please, Mr. Dark, just fuck me!"

He pushed his cock a little deeper, just the head, until I felt my walls give, only a little. I gasped and moaned, excited because I thought he'd finally given in, that he was about to do it.

"Do you know how much I want that, pet? To be inside of you." He gasped when I inhaled sharply. The motion caused me to move down on him, just a centimeter. "But no, the contract must be honored."

He pulled away from me, out of the minute part of me he'd entered, just enough to know what it would feel like, and moved up beside of me. He leaned up on his arm and looked down on me as he stroked his cock.

"I think I'd be inside of you 24-7 if it wasn't for that contract, pet." He paused to inhale through his teeth as pleasure took him. "I have the most filthy fantasies about you, Stephanie. All day long, I think about how I'd like to fuck you over my bed or over a desk. I think about how you'd clamp down on me when you come, ever so prettily for me."

His eyes, so close to mine, were glazed with his need, with the pleasure he was giving himself as he stroked at his length. I knew he just needed a little more to set him off.

"How would you fuck me the first time, Mr. Dark? Tell me?" I ran a finger down his chest and spoke into his ear in a whisper. My fingers found a nipple, and I tweaked it, just a little. I figured if it felt good to me, it might to him. A moan of enjoyment told me I was right. "Maybe I'd have you on your knees first, taking my cock as I fuck you hard and fast. Your breasts would grind into the mattress, teasing your nipples as I pounded into you." He paused, and I watched a shudder go through him. Almost there.

"Tell me more, Mr. Dark," I panted the words and felt my body responding to him all over again. His pleasure turned me on, and I wanted all of it. I wanted to watch him, to see what happened when a man got off.

"You'd take my cock so well. Even as a virgin, I can tell your pussy would be hungry for me. And I'd give it every inch it wanted. You'd be such a good fuck, pet. You'd take my cock like the good girl you are, and you'd milk it dry; I just know you would."

One more thrust and his mouth opened, and his eyes went wide. Almost there. My eyes shifted, from his face to his cock and back again. I wanted to see it all. I bit my lip and stayed quiet as he began to speak again.

"Fuck you're beautiful, pet." He breathed the words as he fisted his cock harder, faster, but almost as if he wasn't aware what he was doing at all. His eyes were glued to mine.

"Come for me, sir." It was a request, not a demand, and he made this sound in the back of his throat like I'd said the most erotic thing ever.

"You want to watch me, pet?" he asked, his hand now a blur. "Promise you'll be mine. Promise I'm the only one who gets that pussy, that it's mine," he growled as he worked himself a little harder, and I glanced down, enthralled with how dark his cock was.

"It's yours, Mr. Dark, only yours!" I watched as the first jet of his come exploded from his cock. It shot onto my belly, a warm surprise. Over and over, he released a flood on me, and somehow this was even more erotic than when he'd come in my mouth.

How would it feel to have him do that inside of me? I was dying to know.

# DYLAN

The next morning, I got out of bed, had a shower, and ordered some breakfast for us both. I slid into the bed in fresh pajamas and pulled Stephanie into my arms. I smiled as she protested and knew I'd made the right decision.

"Wake up, pet. I want to talk to you. I have coffee for you and food." She turned in my arms, warm from her sleep, and protested again.

"But I want to sleep," she mewled, and I laughed again.

"No, enough sleep. Come on, come join me." Her face was against my neck, and her lips felt really nice there, but I had an offer to make, and she needed to be awake for it.

"Fine," she said, a little petulant, but softened it with a smile. I let it pass and went to the table with her.

It was only a small table with two white chairs, and we each took a seat. "What do you want in your coffee?"

"Just cream." The words were garbled on a yawn as she scrubbed at her face with her hands. "Nothing else."

"There you go." I set it in front of her and began to eat the breakfast I'd ordered. Hash browns, bacon, toast, and scrambled eggs. I'd ordered a variety because I didn't know what she'd want. There was even glazed doughnuts, if she wanted those.

I wasn't surprised when she picked one up and began to eat. She'd pinch a bite off and pop it into her mouth, her eyes glued to the plate. I knew it was just because her brain hadn't kicked in yet, and I waited as she slowly ate.

Eventually, her eyes came up to me, and she smiled. Her hair was crazy, tangled and spiky in places, but she was still beautiful. "Good morning."

"Good morning, Stephanie. Are you ready?"

She'd finished one cup of coffee and poured another with a deep breath. "I think so."

"Good. Now…" I paused to draw a stack of paper from the trolley the food had come on and two pens. One red, one black. "This is a new contract. One I hope you'll accept."

"Let me see." She pulled the papers over to her and began to read. Her brows knitted together, and I handed her the red pen.

"If there's something you disagree with, then cross it out with this pen."

She clicked the pen and began to cross things out. So much I thought there wasn't much point in the contract. Until I noticed what she'd crossed out exactly.

"Tell me what you think," I said once she'd finished.

"You said you didn't do contracts for longer than three days." Caught in the lie I hadn't told yet. I'd planned to tell her I did sometimes, but I couldn't lie to her. Something in me wouldn't allow it.

"You're different, that's all I can say." It was an admission I hadn't wanted to make, but she forced it out of me with those eyes that saw everything, even if they didn't always announce what they'd seen.

"I'll accept that. Are you sure two weeks isn't too long?" Those amazing eyes caught mine, and I felt like a bug under a microscope.

"It might be, but I'm confident we'll fill the time well." She made a note on the paper with a black pen. "Are you sure you want to add that?"

"What? The get out of jail free card? Yes. You might get bored." She smiled, but there was a sadness to it.

"Alright. But I don't think a week is long enough. Two weeks should be sufficient." I'd fuck her six ways to Sunday and get her out of my system. I'd hoped.

"Shall I change it back to two then?" Her eyes bored into mine, and I smiled, enamored with her charm.

"Yes, pet."

"Alright. Now, this part where we meet at your house. Are you sure about that?" Again, her eyes were on mine and I couldn't look away.

"I'd rather be in my home when I fuck you the first time, Stephanie. Not here. If that's alright with you."

"Well, I'm not sure about that, to be honest. Being here gives me reassurance, if I'm honest. Not that I think you'll chain me up and never let me go. But here, there's added safety." She looked away, and I knew it was an issue of trust. Fuck, how would I get around that?

"Would you feel safer at your home? I really think your first time should be in a more personal place than what amounts to a brothel, if we're honest about it." I was a little impatient, but I forced myself to reel it in. "I think you deserve more than this, Stephanie."

I leaned over the table and placed my hand over hers. I needed to reassure her, and touch always worked best on her.

"I'm not sure about my place either. Like I said, I feel safer here. No matter what it really is."

I didn't point out the rooms were sound-proofed, and no one would hear her scream if she actually screamed for help. This was an issue, one I hadn't realized would be. I didn't want to take her virginity in a brothel, and she was afraid to leave it. What to do.

"We can work on that later then. What else do you

object to?" I waited for the next objection as her eyes traveled down the page.

"I don't want your money." She looked me right in the eye when she said it. "That is a grotesque amount, and if I'm honest, I've never wanted money. I only took it because it was part of the deal here. The house takes a cut of it."

"Then donate it to a charity." Solved simply enough, I'd thought.

"I'm not sure I should donate money I've earned on my back to charity." She looked ruffled about that, and I knew I could handle this one.

"Then I'll do it for you. Just tell me which charity you want the money to go to." I smiled blandly.

She looked up, her left brow crooked and her lips pursed. "No, you don't get it. I don't want money to fuck you, sir. Any."

"Oh?" Now I was confused.

"I don't want to feel like your whore, sir. I want to feel like your sub. Money makes me feel like I have to perform, put on a show. And for that many zeroes, it would have to be some show. I don't want that." She scratched at the number again, over and over, until the red ink obscured the black numbers.

"Fine. No money, then." I'd still donate something to the charity she'd started to write on the paper and crossed out.

"And, I'm not sure about this…" I saw what she'd pointed at and lifted an eyebrow.

"Are you serious?" Considering where we were, I was a bit surprised at her objection.

"I don't mind if you see my face, but I don't want anyone else to. I won't go out to a place like that without a mask." She had set her jaw and looked me dead in the eye. I knew she wouldn't budge on that.

This only made me suspicious that she came from a very wealthy family, one that she wanted to protect. "Alright then. We'll go in disguise. Make a game of it."

"I can agree to that." She smiled and relaxed.

It was a different club, one that was much wilder than this place, and I wanted to take her to show her the many levels of submission, to see if she found a new one she wanted to explore.

"And this?" she asked with a lifted eyebrow. It was easier to see without the mask, and they were a golden color, so not invisible as some natural blondes were.

"You don't want group sex?" I wasn't surprised about that, but a little disappointed.

"Not with other men. No penetration, at all, from other men." She paused, as if to think about it. "Not right now, anyway."

"Remember, Stephanie, if it goes in the contract, it stays," I warned her with a firm voice. "We don't change anything that we put in here."

Her cheeks flamed red, and she pulled her bottom lip in between her teeth. "Hmm."

"Leave it in then?"

"Let's add the words 'may or may not'. I'd like to keep that possibility open."

"That's fine then." I wouldn't push her into anything like that, but if the opportunity presented itself, well, I didn't want her to miss anything. I'd planned to open a new world to her.

"And this?" I didn't have to look.

"Birth control will be used. I was careless last night, but that won't happen again. I don't want you saddled with a child from an experiment you wanted to engage in. It's not fair to you."

"Thank you." I could see she hadn't really thought about the consequences of what we would soon do, if she agreed to sign the contract, but was now. "I think you're right. This is only for two weeks. It's not a marriage contract."

"Not at all. You shouldn't have to pay a price for it. That ensures I keep my promise to not burden you in such a way."

"Thank you," she said again, then she read through the rest of it. "I'm fine with this. I want to take it deeper, and like you, I don't want to deal with blood. I would like to add one thing, though." She smiled a secret smile then looked up at me. "I want you to be a little rougher, or little more commanding. Not always, but I want to go deeper. Last night was … brilliant, but I want it to last longer. And I want you to use a crop on me."

"As you wish. Just write it down."

The words were put into the contract, and I picked it up from the table. "We'll have this printed up, and it should be ready before you're dressed."

"Alright. I have a meeting I have to attend this afternoon, but after that I'll be yours for the next two weeks. If everything goes to plan."

"I'll have the papers for you to sign shortly. I want you to take it home, really think about it, and then sign it. Do your meeting, and spend the night relaxing. Take time to think about it, and then get back to me, okay?"

"That sounds like a plan."

I stood, kissed her before I left the room, and went to find someone to type the papers up.

It took a little searching, and then I had to wait for the copies to print out, but in all, it only took about a half hour. When I got back to the room, Stephanie was dressed in a pair of tailored dark blue slacks, a white cashmere sweater, and black Prada boots that came up to her knees. The rings and earrings she wore were expensive, not costume jewelry, and there was an elegant way she spoke and carried herself, as if she'd been taught deportment.

"Here's your copy. Let me know tonight what you

want to do, okay?" I pulled her to me and kissed her deeply.

Our breath was fast and rough by the time I pulled away from her. She smiled, wiped at the corner of her mouth, and left me, papers in hand. I'd see her again tomorrow, if everything worked out, though, I didn't see a reason it wouldn't.

Not long after, I left the club and turned on my phone. I checked the messages as soon as I got to the black sports car I'd rented for my time here. I had a call from Liz.

"I've found it, the perfect place, and if you hurry, you can get it in your hands before the Thompsons find out it's even up for sale. Call me."

My heart raced as I got into the car and called Liz back. "Tell me about it."

"It's just what you've been looking for, and the kick in the teeth is it's right beside the Thompsons' hotel. The owner called me last night to find out if I had any connections who would be interested. You immediately crossed my mind." Her voice, always sultry, had an added note of conquest that made her sound even sexier.

"You've done well. Tell me what I need to do."

"You need to get over here right away and sign some papers, then get the money in order. I'm sure Trent will hear about this soon, so you need to get over here like five minutes ago."

"I'm on my way." The day had barely even started, and I'd already made two conquests. It was going to be a good day.

## EMILY

*I* drove to the hotel lazily, a smile fixed on my face that I just couldn't get rid of. Even when the traffic was terrible, I kept smiling as memories played in my head. Mr. Dark wanted me for two more weeks, in a private place, twenty-four hours a day.

That sounded like heaven on earth to me, and I would make sure Trent understood when I saw him that I wasn't to be disturbed, for anything other than a true emergency during that time. I parked and headed into the hotel and up to the offices. I waved at the secretary who waved back as I knocked on the door to the main office.

"I'm here, Trent," I said as I entered and sat on the couch. I felt more confident than I ever had before as I stared at my brother. He was on the phone and hadn't even acknowledged I was there yet.

I waited, impatiently, and didn't make myself stop when my foot began to tap. Always so fucking important, always so dismissive, my brothers could be real assholes sometimes. My smile turned to a glare, and I watched him. He left me sitting there for fifteen minutes, well after the time we'd agreed on for our appointment.

"Fucking Dylan James. Patricidal bastard. He should be in jail, not trying to buy hotels out from under me." I looked up as Trent banged his fist on the desk.

"Pardon?" I blinked and sat up straighter. What was he on about now?

"Dylan James. An asshole from out west who wants to corner the market on the east coast. I won't let him in, but he might have gotten around me this time. Dammit. And to think, he should really be sitting in a jail cell for murdering his parents. Fuck!" Trent banged his fist on the table again, and I glared at him.

"If you're going to keep doing that, I'm going to leave." I wouldn't have said that to him two weeks ago. Now, I knew I could. And I didn't want to hear any more about this man that Trent thought had murdered his parents. I had far more important things to attend to than his little fights with property tycoons.

"Pardon?" he asked, taken aback by my rebuke. Only once in our lives had I ever spoken to him like that, and that was because he'd hurt my best friend's feelings.

He was married to her now, and I rarely saw her, especially now that I wasn't helping out with the kids, but I still loved her. Him, on the other hand, I'd decided, needed to be dealt with.

"Look, why did you ask me here, Trent? I have things to do, you know?" I lifted an eyebrow and glared at him. I could have laughed when his jaw dropped open and his eyebrows shot up.

"Oh, well, I was going to ask you to watch the kids … where are you going?" he called after me when I got up and went to the door.

"Trent, I am your sister. None of you have ever treated me like I am. I know you have the excuse that your mother wasn't my mother, but really? Isn't it time you got past that and treated me with some respect? I love your children, but damn! Enough is enough! No, I won't watch your kids. Hire a fucking nanny!" I was angrier than I'd been when I left the family the first time and came out here. How fucking dare he?

I wasn't normally one for swearing, but I was so mad; I couldn't help it. He'd already forgotten our talk? My demand for respect from them? How could he?

I went to the car, drove home, and had calmed down by the time I got there. I took the packet of papers Mr. Dark had given me into the living room and sat down to go over the lines that had been edited. It was all there in black and white. The plans he had, the things I'd asked to be added in, and the promise of two weeks of pure pleasure.

He would take me places; some I would go into incognito, in others, I'd go as myself. He would also lead me deeper into the lifestyle he'd barely nudged me into. I found I wanted to go deeper with him; I craved the things he'd written down.

I remembered the way he'd slapped my ass and squirmed on my plush sofa. I missed him already. Too bad we hadn't agreed to start right away. I flipped the pages and read about the specific items that he would use on me, the ones I'd agreed to. I wasn't sure what some of them were, but it sounded exciting, and I wanted to explore that with him.

I only had two weeks with him, so we were going to have a lot of time to explore together, but it wasn't a long time in the grand scheme of things. I'd move on after, as would he, and maybe we'd meet again, but right now, I only had two weeks of heaven to look forward to.

I thought I'd be too embarrassed to do much of this, to talk about some of this so openly, but I had done it and talked about it freely with him. He put me at ease, made it comfortable to talk about, and to even demand things. I didn't want to be emotionally scarred when this was all over, but I did want memories that might have to last me a while.

I didn't know that I'd ever be brave enough to do this with anyone else. And that part about groups? I wasn't so sure about that. I'd only wanted him to touch me, and I'd only wanted to touch him. The idea of both being done by someone else did kind of intrigue me, though, I had to admit. That was why I'd capitulated and written in *may or may not engage in activities with others* in that section. Maybe I'd only want to watch or have him watch me.

The idea blossomed in my head, and I sat back on the couch. I imagined him on the other couch, watching as another man settled down between my thighs to do the things he'd done to me. The jealousy I imagined in his eyes started a flame in my blood. I took the fantasy further and imagined him naked. How hard he'd be as he watched another man touch me. Would it really turn him on, I wondered? Would he allow someone else that privilege?

Was that something that would happen in this culture, I had to wonder. I'd be his sub, would he allow that? It was in there in black and white, so he'd have to allow it. I'd realized then just how much freedom he'd given me. Far more than I'd thought I'd have if he'd allow that to happen. The fantasy returned, and my body throbbed with desire.

His eyes would narrow when I put my hands in the

man's hair, as I shivered with pleasure, our eyes would lock together. I added a woman, on her knees, and the fantasy became something totally different. It became something I'd wanted but wasn't sure I'd ever act on. Things like that changed dynamics. I'd seen a movie recently about people who actually acted on those desires, and it hadn't ended well for them. Others online had said it enhanced their relationships, but would it really? I had to wonder, and right now, it was easy to see the good side of it.

Pleasure for both, as we watched the partner we shared be pleasured. I could feel a throb between my thighs, and no amount of squirming on the couch would make it better. I sat up, told myself to be a big girl, and take control. I took a deep breath, went into the kitchen for a glass of apple juice, and came back to finish reading.

There were a few lines about after care and how he'd make sure I was in a fit state at all times. Even when I was on my knees begging, sobbing for relief, he'd make sure I wasn't hurt by the ordeal. Not physically, anyway. But that was the purpose wasn't it, denial to make the proper moment even more explosive?

I knew I was new to all of this BDSM stuff, but I'd done my homework. I knew what I was in for; I just hadn't experienced most of it. Yet. I would soon, very soon.

A text came from Trent, and I stared down at the phone. Was it an apology, or was he upbraiding for speaking to him like that, as if I was a servant? I decided then to get a new phone and only give Mr. Dark the number. My family would be cut out of my life for the next two weeks. Surely nothing too horrible would happen in that time.

I picked up the contract again and turned to the very last page. There, it was stated the contract was not legally binding, not in a court of law, but we would be expected to treat the contract as if it was. He'd already signed it, and I loved the scrawl of his name. It was legible, but showy, a little bit like him.

I took the paper and started to sign it when I finally noticed his real name was under the scrawl. My heart thudded in my chest, and I felt the world narrow down to those two names.

Dylan. James.

Fuck.

No, there was no way I could sign that contract now. The fantasies crumbled, and the joy that had filled me up vanished in an instant. My brother's nemesis. My family's nemesis. I'd been sleeping with the enemy, quite literally.

I stared at the contract, everything suddenly changed. My hands shook as I put it down and pushed myself into the edge of the sofa. I needed comfort, and there was no one here who could do it. I could call Roxie, talk to her, but what would that solve? Jesse was always busy with being a wife and mother now; I couldn't call her either. Besides, I'd have to admit what I'd been doing to her, and right now, I didn't want to do that.

The very thing I'd wanted most, that had been just within my reach, was now totally out of my hands. I couldn't go through with it, after all. It would be a betrayal of my family. If they ever found out, they'd never forgive me. It would be the end of our relationship. And Trent had said Dylan had killed his parents. I dismissed that as a bold-faced lie, right away. The man I knew would never do something like that.

Sure, he'd consider chaining me down to a table and torturing me with pleasure, but he wasn't a killer. I'd caught the tail-end of that fight last night but had left it unmentioned in the excitement of our reunion. Mr. Dark, Dylan, was a protector, not a killer. I couldn't believe that for a minute.

I'd heard Trent complain about him a few times now that I'd thought about it. He'd come to Myrtle Beach looking for property, a resort to grow his family's business. That wasn't so wrong, was it? My thoughts started to turn. Just because Trent wanted to play a game of 'whose dick is bigger' didn't mean I'd have to give this up. Did it?

I pulled my legs up close and wrapped my arms around them as I thought about it. If I kept my identity secret, kept up the fake name and made sure he didn't find out who I was, he'd never know, would he? He didn't have to know I was a Thompson, at all. Ever.

Maybe I could make this work. It would mean an amendment to the contract, or maybe a verbal agreement, but he'd have to agree to never seek me out once this was all done and over with. And he'd only be able to take me places I knew people wouldn't know me. That wasn't too hard around here; I'd rarely gone out here, but people did know me from my charity work.

Shit. What about that? God, this was all stupid!

I was a grown woman. I should be able to do as I please. But family was important to me, even if I was angry at them all right now. This would shame our family if it got out, and I'd have to work really hard to make sure it was never known. But if we went out in public, then there was a possibility that would happen.

I could already picture the disappointment on their faces, the shock, and maybe the disgust. Was it worth it?

I remembered the way he touched me, the exquisite sensation of his hand against my ass as he worked those pumps on me, and I heard myself moan. It was worth it, oh, it was worth it.

I bit my lip and played through every moment I could think of. How he'd made me feel powerful and helpless at the same time. How he'd given me pleasure that far surpassed anything I could have imagined. The way his face softened when he came and how much he wanted to fuck me.

But could I? Could I look him in the eye knowing my brother wanted to keep him from gaining a foothold in Myrtle Beach? That it was my family who had nearly driven him mad over the last few weeks as he tried to find property and was turned away at every point? It was my family that had done that.

Would he use it against me? Shit, I hadn't thought about that. Would he even want to fuck me if he knew who I was? Or would he do it and then crow about it to get back at my family? Maybe that was why he'd changed my mind. Or was it my own self-doubt? No, there was no way he could have figured out who I was.

I picked up the contract and tapped it against my leg. He'd given me tonight to think about it. I'd planned to sign it, call Roxie, and wait for the next day impatiently. Now, the scenario had changed, reality had changed. Last night, when he'd made me come with a shuddering scream, he'd been a stranger, a man that I couldn't get enough of, but someone safe who didn't threaten me in any way.

Now, he was the man that could destroy my world and tear my family apart. I had no idea what to do. I wanted him, but could I take the consequences if our affair was found out? Would my family ever forgive me? Would he if he found out who I really was? I picked up the phone. I needed to talk to someone, but there was no one to call. I had to make this decision all on my own.

# TWISTED INTENTION
~ A billionaire revenge romance series ~
Twisted Beauty
Twisted Love
Twisted Fate

## Mafia's Obsession
~ A hot mafia romance series ~
Mafia's Dirty Secret
Mafia's Fake Bride
Mafia's Final Play

## Screaming Demons
~ An MC romance series full of suspense ~
Rough Start
Rough Ride
Rough Choice
Rough Patch
Rough Return
Rough Road
Rough Trip
Rough Night
Rough Love

## Standalone Contemporary Romance
Billionaire in Vegas
Billionaire Hunt

Billionaire's Game
Billionaire Retreat
Billionaire On Air
A Chance To Love
Somebody To Love
Not Mine To Love

Check out Summer's entire collection at
**www.summercooper.com/books**

# ABOUT SUMMER COOPER

Thank you so much for reading. Without you, it wouldn't be possible for me to be a full-time author. I hope you enjoy reading my books as much as I do writing them.

Besides (obviously!) reading and writing, I also love cuddling my dogs, shouting at Alexa, being upside down (aka Yoga) and driving my family cray-cray!

Get in touch at
hello@summercooper.com
www.summercooper.com

facebook.com/summercooperauthor
instagram.com/summercooperauthor
goodreads.com/summercooper
bookbub.com/profile/summer-cooper